D0648751

MARIKE'S
WORLD

Also by Catherine M. Rae

Sunlight on a Broken Column

The Hidden Cove

Flight from Fifth Avenue

The Ship's Clock

Afterward

Sarah Cobb

Julia's Story

Brownstone Facade

MARIKE'S WORLD

Catherine M. Rae

INDIANAPOLIS MARION CO.

PUBLIC LIBRARY

THOMAS DUNNE BOOKS
St. Martin's Press
New York

THOMAS DUNNE BOOKS.
An imprint of St. Martin's Press.

MARIKE'S WORLD. Copyright © 2000 by the Estate of Catherine M. Rae.
All rights reserved. Printed in the United States of America. No part
of this book may be used or reproduced in any manner whatsoever
without written permission except in the case of brief quotations
embodied in critical articles or reviews. For information, address
St. Martin's Press, 175 Fifth Avenue, New York, N.Y. 10010.

www.stmartins.com

Design by Heidi M. Eriksen

Library of Congress Cataloging-in-Publication Data

Rae, Catherine M., date
    Marike's world / Catherine M. Rae—1st ed.
        p. cm.
    ISBN 0-312-26199-3
    1. New York (N.Y.)—History—Revolution, 1775–1783—Fiction.
    2. Young women—Fiction.   I. Title.

PS3568.A355 M37 2000
813'.54—dc21

                                                    00-028581

First Edition: July 2000

10 9 8 7 6 5 4 3 2 1

For Larry

January 13, 1809

My dear, dear Margretta,

When you brought your children to see me on New Year's Day you asked me what life was like when I was a girl. I tried to tell you about it, my daughter, to paint a few little pictures for you, but after you left I realized how inadequate my words were and that what I really wanted to do was to give you a complete picture of my early life.

I have, therefore, written this account of my girlhood, when I was still Marike Dykeman, and of my young womanhood. It is easier for me to put it down on paper than to speak the words. Believe me, my darling, that what I have written here is the truth; you must not listen to anyone who tells you otherwise.

I shall put these pages safely away for you to read at some future date. Now is not the time.

—Mama

Chapter One

I can never look back on the terrible fire of 1776, the one that destroyed hundreds of houses as well as Trinity Church, as a blessing, but in a way it was one for me. It saved me not only from the wrath of my parents but also from the ignominy of public disgrace. Of course there were those few (there are always some who suspect something other than what they are told) who treated me cautiously, as if I were not wholly trustworthy, which I guess I am not when you come right down to it.

During the two years that preceded the fire New York was in a state of unrest, so much so that the grown-ups, even those not engaged in city affairs, were on edge and short-tempered. My brothers, Jan and Pieter, and I found it best to follow parental orders promptly and to keep out of the way as much as possible. This was not always easy to do, since the duties assigned to us often involved our father and mother. The boys were working with Papa, helping to build the rows of small houses that were

3

spreading out to the north of us, and after I was taken out of the Dame's School up on Prince Street (where I learned to read and to write a fair hand, and which I was loath to leave) most of my day was taken up with domestic chores: churning the butter, making the cheese, scrubbing the tiles in the kitchen, and cleaning, cleaning, cleaning. Even the road in front of our house on Beaver Street had to be swept, and every Friday I was out there with a broom, whisking the dirt and trash into piles, which would be taken away later by the men who came around with their carts. If the mistress of a Dutch household had a passion for anything it was for cleanliness; she cleaned everything she owned, and Mama was no exception. She kept at it and kept me at it until we were both exhausted, or until it was time to sit down and pick up the mending or our knitting.

By the time I was twelve I could turn out a pair of woolen stockings almost as good as the ones my mother's flashing needles produced, and a year later I was able to adorn them with the bright-colored clocks the boys liked. If we weren't knitting, we were mending, or patching trousers, skirts, petticoats, or shirts, whatever needed repair. None of us had extensive wardrobes; what clothes we had we kept until they were thoroughly worn out, at which point they would be carefully cut into squares for dustings (flannel petticoats were good for these) or into strips to be made into rag rugs. We wasted nothing. It never occurred to me to complain about having so few clothes; I simply wore the same woolen skirts over two (or three on bitter-cold days) petticoats in winter and in summer high-necked gingham or calico dresses, sometimes with a fichu that covered the bodice and was crossed at the waist.

Occasionally I would see the governor's lady and some of her friends driving out in their carriages and marvel at the beauty of their silks and satins, but did I envy them? No. They had what they had and we had what we had; it was as simple as that. Envy would have complicated things.

I was happiest, I think, on the days I went to Mistress Shelby's house on Anne Street to deliver some knitting or mending Mama had done for the old lady. It was there, in the cluttered front room of Mistress Shelby's tiny house that I learned to appreciate the beauty of the English language.

Mistress Shelby spoke slowly and precisely, pronouncing each word carefully, and one day when she caught me imitating her she smiled and asked if I would like to improve my vocabulary.

"I will make you a list of words, my dear," she said, taking up a quill pen and beginning to write. "I will explain their meanings, and you must get them by heart. Then the next time you come we will discuss them and use them in sentences. Will you do that for me?"

I loved doing it, and for the next three years, until poor Mistress Shelby died of some fever or other, I seized every opportunity to hurry over to Anne Street, carrying something Mama had baked or sewed, sure of a delightful hour with my elderly friend.

A boring life, I imagine I hear you say, and you would be right; for the most part it was deadly dull. There were, however, some compensations: an occasional party, outing, or wedding to attend, or even something as simple as helping with the picking of ripe fruit, which would provide an opportunity for a young girl like me, Marike Dykeman, to be with people her own age.

One late summer day in particular stands out in my memory: it was when I was seventeen years old and people were beginning to comment on how pretty I was becoming when Jan, Pieter, and I went over to the Wiltwyck farm to help bring in the pear crop. Mama was pleased to let us go because she knew Vrouw Wiltwyck would send us home with our string bags filled with enough fruit to make a good supply of pear brandy, and Papa approved of anything that produced tangible results. If they knew about the horseplay and flirtations that went on under the pear trees, and I am reasonably sure they did, they said nothing beyond warning us to behave ourselves and to be home before sunset. Then Mama handed over the food I had helped pack and sent us off.

We had rather a long walk to the orchard, a couple of miles, I think. Because of all the building going on in lower New York farmers were forced to move to the north, and according to Papa the time would come when there wouldn't be a single farm or orchard left in Manhattan. He was right, of course, but I hated the way he said things like that, as if he were God Himself making an announcement.

Yes indeed, he was right. The Wiltwyck orchard is long gone, replaced by rows of tidy brick and brownstone houses, but I have no trouble picturing it as it was that warm, sunny day, the day I met Philip Bogardus. I could not help but notice him, a tall, slender young man dressed in a light blue shirt and a pair of dark britches that seemed to emphasize the shapeliness of his long legs. When I realized that he had glanced over in my direction more than once I wondered whether he would speak to me, but he said nothing until a wasp stung me and I uttered a sharp little cry.

"What is it?" he asked, hurrying over to where I stood staring at the swelling on my wrist. "Oh, a sting. You'll need some mud to put on it."

He picked up a stick and scraped a bit of dirt from the base of the tree.

"This is too dry," he said, holding it out to me, "but if you smear it on your wrist it will help take the sting out until I come back with some water. Wait here."

He disappeared in the direction of the barn and returned a few minutes later carrying a wet handkerchief from which he squeezed a few drops of water onto my wrist.

"Oh, it feels better," I said gratefully, "so much better. But now your handkerchief is all wet."

"No matter," he said with a laugh. "I'll just put it around my neck to keep me cool. That's why I brought it with me."

After that it seemed only natural that he should help me with the pears that were too high up in the tree for me to reach, and even more natural for us to sit together in the shade and share our food when the gong sounded at midday. I had brought the usual bread and cheese, along with a slice of cold venison and two of Mama's olykoeks, or oilcakes, delicious little confections flavored with chopped apple, citron, and raisins. I gave him one of the cakes and in return he handed me a square of gingerbread he said their cook had made.

"You have a better cook than we do, Marike," he said, savoring the last crumbs of the oilcake. "Is she a slave? Ours tries hard, but she doesn't do too well."

I was surprised that a boy who came from a household that kept a slave—only a few of the wealthier families did so—would be out picking pears, but I merely smiled and said that my mother and I did the cooking.

After we had finished off our meal with a couple of ripe pears, the juice of which helped assuage our thirst, I leaned against the trunk of the nearest tree and Philip stretched out on the grass nearby while we waited for the signal to resume picking. I could hear the murmur of voices and an occasional burst of laughter from other pickers, but nothing disturbed the sensation of excited tranquility (if there is such a thing) that came over me as I listened to Philip's pleasant voice and watched his face crinkle up when he laughed. I think I knew then that I would love him. I'm almost sure I did.

Tired as I was by the time the sun began to sink low in the sky, I didn't want the afternoon to end. I wanted to go on talking to Philip and listening to him tell about life in the Bogardus household, which was evidently ruled by a father as stern and strict as mine. I guess most Dutch fathers were like that then. Maybe they are still.

"I'm almost ready, Marike," Philip said, bending a high branch down so that I could reach the pears on it, "almost ready to strike out on my own. I'll be twenty next month, old enough to make my own rules and decisions, but first I must find some means of supporting myself. So far I have worked only under my father's direction."

"So have my brothers," I said. "They work with Papa building houses. Today he gave them a holiday, but tomorrow they will have to work harder and longer to make up for it. What kind of work does your father do?"

"He has a ship chandler's shop on South Street," he answered. "He sells things the sailing ships need, mostly English ships these days. He's had it ever since I can remember. He'd been in the Dutch navy, a supply officer, until he was hurt and could no longer go to sea. He doesn't complain, but he's had a stiff leg and pains and aches ever since."

"How did he get hurt?" I asked when Philip paused. "Was he at sea when it happened?"

"No, they were in port, loading the ship, when a heavy cask filled with fresh water rolled over on him. No one expected him to live, but he did, and when he was well enough he collected his pay and came here. He went to work for Herr Van Osler, who owned the chandlery, and when the old man died Papa took it over and made it into the successful business it is today."

"Did he meet your mother in Holland?" I asked, wondering whether they'd come to America together.

"Ah, no," Philip sighed. "That's another story, and not a happy one. Papa sent for his parents after a while and supported them until they died. But he met my mother here. She lived with her family up near the Zuyder Zee. When she was five years old, or maybe six, marauding Indians raided their little village, and apparently she saw her mother and father killed. She escaped by hiding in the woods, where a family named Bemberg found her. They took her in and brought her up. Years later my father met her at some church affair and married her. I think they've been happy, even though my mother is an extremely nervous and excitable woman. Papa told me she'd never recovered from seeing what happened to her parents, and I believe it. She still goes into hysterics every time she sees an Indian."

"Even the friendly ones who come here to sell fish and animal skins?"

"Yes, I'm afraid so, but my sisters and I know that she can't help it, and run for her potion to calm her. It seems to work."

"And you, Philip, what will you do if you leave the chandlery?"

"I could stay there," he answered slowly, "or I could go to sea any time I liked, and I won't say I haven't been tempted, but . . ."

Here he hesitated for a moment or two. Then after absent-mindedly tossing a pear into my basket he continued slowly: "I think I'd rather be a landsman, have a farm, children, maybe even a pear orchard," he finished with a laugh.

A few minutes later one of the Wiltwyck sons came by in a cart drawn by a farm horse and began to collect what we had picked. He was a big, cheerful fellow, and strong, who lifted the heavy baskets as if they were filled with feathers.

"There's cider for you in the barn," he shouted. "Papa says to have a cup or two before you go. It's nice and cold. Tastes good on a hot day."

It did taste good. I should say here that none of us ever expected to be paid for our work in the orchard; fruit picking was looked upon, at least by us young people, as recreation, a respite from the ordinary day's occupation, and considered a cup of cider or two ample reward.

I was ready to start for home, and after Vrouw Wiltwyck had filled my bag with fruit from the pile she had set aside for the pickers (not the very best pears, I noticed) Philip offered to carry it for me.

"Then I will know where you live," he said, keeping his eyes averted. "I should like to come and see you some evening, Marike. We could go over to the river, perhaps, and watch the boats and waterfowl."

He frowned slightly as he spoke, but when I assured him

that I would like to do that he smiled and took my hand in his free one.

For the remaining days of that summer and all during the following fall and winter Philip was a constant visitor to our modest home. To my surprise neither of my parents made any objection to his presence, since they'd both been highly critical of the few young men who'd called on me in the past. Papa had even threatened Gerard Vanderbeck with a beating if he ever came near the house again. As far as I could tell all poor Gerard had done was to refer to the tavernkeeper as a bloodsucker and despoiler, which to Papa constituted "foul and villainous" language. Philip, on the other hand, was soft-spoken, courteous, and not unwilling to lend a hand with some of the heavier chores. Pieter and Jan teased me about him, but I could tell from the way they acted that they held nothing against him.

Perhaps I had no right to be as happy as I was that year when all the Dutch families, at least all the ones we knew, were constantly complaining about the hardships they endured under British rule, but what girl in love for the first time in her life could be anything but happy? I had a tall, handsome lover with soft blond hair that curled around his ears and at the nape of his neck, and eyes as blue as the summer sky, so much more beautiful than my own nondescript gray ones. How could I not be head over heels in love with him, and how could I worry about the future of the city when all my thoughts were directed toward a life with Philip on the farm he would own, to our lives together in the house I would run for him? He would ask Papa for my hand, he said, as soon as he saw his way clear to acquiring the land he'd had his eye on for several months.

"It's over on Long Island, Marike, where the soil is good and crops and orchards will flourish," he said, gazing off into the distance as if visualizing an established farm. Then his expression changed and he frowned slightly as he continued: "I hope you won't be lonely there, my darling. It will be some distance from your family, and there won't be any close neighbors."

"I'll have you, Philip. How could I be lonely? And in time we'll have our own family," I said, letting my head rest on his shoulder while he untied the drawstring at the neck of my dress. We were quiet after that, happily quiet. Later, when I was in bed, I thought about how gentle and tender he was when he held me and kissed me and how all too soon it was time for me to go home and for him to run off into the darkness.

As the spring advanced toward summer and the days lengthened we had more time to ourselves than we'd had during the cold, snowy winter, and Philip's expression of his love for me grew more and more exciting. He'd take me to a secluded place on the bank of the Hudson or to a field of tall grasses, and we'd lie close together, caressing each other and murmuring words of love for as long as I dared stay away from home. No one came near us, but occasionally we'd catch sight of other courting couples, who, like us, were too intent upon themselves to interfere with anyone else's lovemaking.

"This is wonderful," I whispered to Philip one evening. "Can it last? Can we possibly go on being this happy?"

"Oh, yes we can, my little love," he answered, letting his

hands move gently over my body. "Not only will it last, but it will get better and better, more wonderful. You'll see. Look at me, Marike; kiss me—there, that's better. No, no, don't pull away from me. Come closer. I need you."

That was the night he gave me the ring I have cherished all these years. When we stood up to leave the quiet spot by the river he held me close to him for a few moments, then, releasing me, he smiled and reached into one of his pockets.

"I was so busy loving you, my darling, that I nearly forgot this," he said, handing me a tiny sack made of soft, faded flannel and tied with a drawstring of old blue ribbon. I opened it carefully, and when I saw the little silver ring it contained I couldn't speak; I simply stood still and stared at it.

"My grandmother (she made us all call her Grossmoeder) gave it to me shortly before she died," Philip said in a voice that seemed to come from far away. "She said it no longer fitted on her finger, and that I was to give it to the maiden I wanted to marry."

"Oh, Philip!" I finally exclaimed. "A silver ring! I never had a ring in my life! And look, it has my initial on it!"

"Yes, love, her name was Marthe. Seems as if it was meant for you."

"See, it fits my finger—"

"Yes, but you must not wear it now. I have not yet spoken to your father."

"But Philip—oh, I know; I'll pin it inside my bodice. No one will see it there, and I will have it with me all the time."

Later, when I asked him why his grandmother had not given it to his mother, he said the two women had never liked each other, but he didn't say why. Perhaps he didn't know. In any

13

case, I didn't really care; I was too wrapped up in my own happiness—in spite of the worrying thought that it was too good to last. I should have paid more attention to that thought: it *was* too good to go on and on, and before long several events occurred that put an end to our summer idyll.

News of the Declaration of Independence reached us on the ninth of July, 1776, causing great excitement and many celebrations. It also prompted our soldiers to tear down the statue of George the Third and terrify us with their rioting and violence. Our own soldiers! Only after a stern rebuke from General Washington, who had recently made New York his headquarters, was order restored. Then, on the twelfth of July, Admiral Howe's fleet sailed into the harbor and British troops were landed at Gravesend Bay, far too close for comfort.

It was during the weeks that followed this last event that I noticed a definite change in Philip. He spent fewer evenings with me, and when he did come he seemed to be interested in military matters almost to the exclusion of everything else. Of course the spirit of patriotism was running high, especially after Washington withdrew his troops from Long Island and brought them to New York to reorganize, so I guess I shouldn't have been surprised at Philip's announcement. I was, though; I was thunderstruck one evening in early September when he told me the general needed men, and that he, Philip, intended to join him in the fight against the British.

"I wouldn't ever rest easy in my mind if I didn't go, Marike love," he said. "He needs me. He needs every man able to fight. He's a great man and a great leader; I'd do anything for him. Look, my darling, we'll chase the British out and I'll be back before long. You'll be proud of me; you'll know I was never a coward and you'll love me all the more."

Those were his words as I remember them; perhaps they are not just what he said, but almost. I was more than a little upset at the time because I was wondering how to tell him that I might be with child. In the end I said nothing.

Chapter Two

For a while I hoped against hope that I was mistaken, but as the early fall days slipped by with no sign of my monthly flow I became almost frantic with worry. How long could I keep my condition hidden? Would I be turned out of the house when my secret was discovered? Where would I go, and what would become of my baby? Oh, how I longed for Philip! How I wished he hadn't gone away. . . .

Acting as if everything were all right was hard; Mama had sharp eyes, and I was terrified she'd see something in my behavior that would make her suspect what was wrong with me, so I tied on my apron and threw myself into the household chores with as much vigor as I could command. Perhaps, though, she was too much concerned with my brothers to pay much attention to me. Pieter and Jan were having constant arguments with Papa at that time because they, too, wanted to join Washington's army, and my father was adamant in refusing to give his permission. When the three of them were at home the atmosphere was heavy, with meals eaten either in sullen silence or accompanied by angry shouts and threats. Neither Mama nor I dared offer an opinion. One look at Papa's face was enough to make us hold our tongues, but my brothers were braver. They argued with Papa. They finally did go off to fight, but that came later on.

I kept wondering where Philip was. Then on September seventeenth we heard that Washington's army had defeated the British in a battle at Harlem Heights. At that point I began to look for his return, but when he neither came back nor sent any word it took all my strength not to surrender to despondency. A bad time, a very bad time.

About a week later, I think it was on the twenty-sixth of September, a dreadful fire broke out in Whitehall Slip and spread quickly over the lower part of the city. Trinity Church burned to the ground, and more than five hundred houses were completely destroyed. It was said later that the shift in the wind that caused St. Paul's Church and Kings College to be spared the flames also allowed our little group of houses to remain standing.

As if the fire hadn't been enough of a calamity, that same day the British captured Nathan Hale, a spy for General Washington, and the British general had him hanged someplace over near the East River.

In the days that followed, while the city continued to function (unhappily, I must say) under British rule, no one paid any attention to me, for which I was grateful. We Dutch were all trying to live quietly, reasoning that the more infrequently we came to the notice of the British the better off we'd be. Jan and Pieter came home with stories of riots caused by the oppression of civilians by British soldiers, and tales of how people everywhere were complaining about the the lack of order, shortage of supplies, and the quartering of British troops in various houses. It was indeed a wretched time, and I was by no means the only person to be close to despair.

"It is true," Papa said one night as we sat in the front room with the shutters closed and the doors bolted, "that there are rowdy troops of men and boys roaming about the streets, and I do not think it is safe for womenfolk to be out of doors these days. Marike, you are to stay in the house with your mother. Jan and Pieter and I can take care of ourselves, but you—they would overpower you in seconds."

Mama and I nodded our heads in assent to his ruling, but I wondered how we would manage without certain daily necessities. I glanced at my mother and knew that in spite of her expression of calm obedience that she already had some plan of her own. I was right: she said nothing that night, but the next morning when Papa and the boys were safely out of the house she sent me to buy the buttermilk she needed for her baking.

"Surely, daughter," she said as she handed me the milk pail and a few coins, "surely this early in the morning there will be no ruffians about. They will all be sleeping off the excesses of last night. Go quickly, Marike, and do not stop on the way and you will be safe. Oh, yes, and see if Vrouw Birkow will let you have a few eggs."

We had dealt with the same dairy for years, and since Mama and vrouw were friends of long standing, I was quite sure of returning with both the buttermilk and a clutch of eggs. Mindful of Papa's warning, I kept an eye out for marauders, but few people were to be seen at that hour and after a while I relaxed my vigilance and began to enjoy the fresh October air. Had I been more careful, more alert, the event that led me to tell the lie that saved my reputation and also had a lasting effect on my life would never have occurred.

This is what happened: the ordinary route to the dairy would have taken me down streets lined with neat little houses like our own, but that morning I decided to follow a narrow lane along which Philip and I had lingered the previous summer. I knew it ended near Vrouw Birkow's house, but what I did not know was that part of it skirted what was now a devastated area, the result of the September fire. Flimsy shacks and canvas tents now occupied the ground where solidly built houses, shops, and stables once stood.

I had paused to take a longer look at the ruined area, shocked at the thought of people living in such a miserable place, when I was startled by the sudden appearance of two roughly dressed men—or maybe they were just big boys—not five feet away from me.

"Ho there!" one of them shouted. "Takin' a look at Canvastown, are ye?"

"Grab 'er, Jed!" the second one cried. "Likely she's got some siller."

I turned to run, but it was too late. They caught me at once, and when I struggled to free myself they threw me to the ground, facedown, so hard that for a moment or two I could see nothing. I heard them laughing and chortling when they found the coins Mama had given me, and I lay still, hoping that now they'd leave me alone, but when I felt hands going up under my skirt and petticoat I screamed and kicked and thrashed around like a madwoman.

Suddenly the one who was holding me down let go of my arms and began to shout:

"Away, Rory, away! Comes som'un!"

Someone or something frightened them off, but when I sat up I could see only a boy with a wheelbarrow, and he was some distance away. My face hurt; I was sure it was scraped and bruised, and my nose bled, but otherwise I seemed to be unhurt. After a while I stood up and started slowly on my way home.

I would have hurried but I needed time to concoct the story that would, I hoped, save me from both private and public disgrace. I had no way of knowing whether a lie would do me more harm than the truth, but I do know that at the time it seemed to be a way, the only way, out of my difficulty.

Mama was standing on our stoop as I approached the house. I could see that she paused in her sweeping of the stone steps when she caught sight of me, and even now, if I close my eyes I can still picture her as she looked that morning, fresh and neat in her everyday clothes. Her long-sleeved bodice fitted her perfectly, and the white kerchief she wore over her shoulders lay in carefully aligned folds. Her skirt came down almost to her ankles, and the apron that covered most of it had been freshly laundered. So neat, so clean . . .

I began to hurry when I was close enough for her to see the sorry state of my own clothes, and as her expression changed from one of welcome to one of dismay I felt the scratches on my face begin to sting from the tears I could no longer hold back.

"Marike! Daughter! What has happened to you?" she cried, ushering me quickly into the house.

"They took the money," I sobbed, "even the milk pail, and

then—they pushed me down on the ground and—oh, Mama, I cannot tell you what they did to me!"

"You must tell me, child. I must know. What did they do? Did they hurt you? Did they violate you?"

She made it easy for me to speak the lie I had rehearsed on my way home.

"Yes," I sobbed. "They hurt me, soiled me. Not just one of them, both of them. What am I to do? Oh, Mama, what am I to do?"

"Maybe you will have to do nothing, daughter," she said soothingly. "It does not always result in a babe. But come now, you must wash yourself. I will show you. Then we will have to wait. We will know by the end of the month."

"But Papa, does Papa have to know?"

"It is better, yes, it is better that we tell him. That way there will be no need to pretend."

If she only knew, I thought, if she only knew.

When I lay in bed that night I could hear my father's deep, angry voice through the closed doors of the bedrooms, and the sound made me tremble. He would be angry at Mama for sending me on that errand, and in a towering rage at me for going by the lane instead of by the regular route. I hardly slept at all that night, and it was with no small amount of fear and trepidation that I went down to breakfast the next morning. Papa said nothing then, however; I do not think he even looked at me, but that night after the supper dishes had been put away he sent the others out of the kitchen and closed the door.

"Sit down, daughter," he said, motioning to the chair opposite his.

I braced myself for a torrent of angry words, but when he spoke again his voice was soft.

"I have control over my anger now," he said slowly, "and I want you to listen carefully to what I have to say. You disobeyed me, Marike, in going to fetch the buttermilk, and I was ready to punish you as you deserved, but I think now, after reflection, that in doing what you did you were only obeying your mother, and I had to ask myself this: what does a wrong and a right add up to? I do not know the answer to that, but I do know this: your action has caused a serious problem for us."

He sighed and sat staring across the room for a minute or two before speaking again.

"Tell me, would you recognize those two ruffians if you saw them again?"

"I don't know, Papa. I did not see their faces clearly. They were big, I know that, and their clothes were ragged. They were dirty, too. Oh, I did hear their names. One was Jed and he called the other one Rory."

The moment I mentioned the two names I regretted volunteering that information. If they were ever found they would simply deny molesting me—but would they be believed, or would I?

"There is probably little hope of finding them," Papa said, shaking his head, "and even if we did they would blame it on you. No, I see only one thing to do if you should find yourself with child, Marike: I shall send you to my brother's farm up north on the Hudson, away from the city. Franz and Tante Greta would take good care of you, and after the child is born we will see what is to be done. If this should ever become known who would have you for his wife? It must be kept quiet, surely you can see that. I shall give the matter further thought, and you are not to question whatever decision I make."

Chapter Three

B y the first week in November, when there was no longer any doubt about my condition, Papa acted quickly. He wrote to his brother Franz and arranged for Mama and me to travel to the farm, which was near a place called Ossining. Hans Grenzer, one of Papa's workmen, would drive us in the wagon generally used for hauling lumber.

"I have heard from Franz," he said one night after supper, "and you are expected. You leave here tomorrow at dawn; no one will see you go at that hour. It will be cold, so dress in your warmest clothes."

With that he turned away, as if he could not bear to look at me for another minute.

"What are we going to do with the child?" Mama moaned as the wagon jolted over the ruts in the road that ran alongside the Hudson River. "Who will ever believe that you—"

"Mama, please, please stop!" I all but shouted.

Startled by my outburst—I had never raised my voice to her before—she stared at me for a moment or two, but she remained quiet.

"I will keep the baby, Mama," I said after a few minutes, "and when Philip comes back and we are married—yes, he has asked me to be his wife—we will bring the child up as one of ours."

"But what if Philip is killed in the fighting?" she asked, frowning at me. "And what if he won't marry you when he learns?"

"He loves me, Mama, and I know he'll marry me. He said he'd come back to me and that we'd have a farm out on Long Island, and Philip is a man of his word."

We had little to say to each other as our journey alongside the cold, gray waters of the river continued. The day itself was cold and gray, with the threat of snow in the heavy clouds. At one point we saw three ships making their way northward, and Hans Grenzer said they were British warships.

As I watched them melt into the wintry distance I wondered again about Philip. Would he survive the rigors of the coming season as Washington's army struggled to defeat the better-equipped British in battle after battle? We had heard how poorly outfitted the Continental soldiers were, and we were not surprised to learn that many of them would be abandoning the great general when their year of duty ended in January. Philip's year would not end until next August, but if the war continued . . .

These and other worrisome thoughts occupied me as I huddled under the coarse blanket, cold and miserable, unable to find a comfortable position on the hard wooden seat. Suddenly I was aware of gunfire in the area to our right, and when I glanced at my mother's white face and saw how her mittened hands fumbled as she tried to adjust the blanket I knew I must do something to allay her fears before she swooned.

"Hans," I called out to the driver, "they are far away, the soldiers who are shooting, aren't they?"

"*Ja,*" he answered, nodding his head vigorously as he urged the horses on with his whip. "Far away, way off."

"See, Mama," I said, taking her hand in mine and nodding toward the forest on our right, "see how deep those woods are. Soldiers would never come through them. The fighting—Papa told us this—is done in open places. We are safe, Mama, we are safe here. Hans, do we get to that town—what is it—Ossining? Do we arrive there soon?

"*Ja,* soon now, soon," he answered.

"See, Mama, we will be—"

Her scream coincided with a shout from Hans as he brought the wagon to a sudden stop and jumped down from his seat. Rising to my feet I was able to see that he was rushing to the aid of someone, man or boy, I could not tell which, who lay directly in our path.

The moment my mother understood what had happened her entire being underwent a complete change; gone was the trembling, frightened creature of a moment ago, and in its place the strong, confident woman I had known all my life. She was in the road, leaning over the figure lying there, and giving orders to Hans while I was still climbing out of the wagon.

"Get a blanket, Hans," she cried. "Hurry! Hurry! See how his arm bleeds! He needs warmth. Marike, come help me wrap him. The poor Indian! He's but a boy."

"But what, what do we do with him?" a bewildered Hans asked.

27

"We put him in the wagon," Mama replied. "Help me, both of you. Help me lift him, gently, gently."

"We cannot take him," Hans protested.

"We cannot leave him to suffer and die," Mama said sharply. "A poor Indian boy who has naught to do with the fighting, either British or American. Come, put him down in the back of the wagon, Hans. Marike, you and I will ride there and hold him. Come! Move quickly!"

The boy, he looked to be about sixteen or seventeen, shuddered as we lifted him into the wagon, but he made no sound as we settled him with his head in my lap and Mama's steadying hands on the wounded arm.

Had there been anyone to see us as we traveled along, he would have thought we made a strange sight, with a disgruntled driver up in front talking to himself (swearing, I think) and two women in the flat part of the wagon crooning softly to a figure wrapped up in a blanket. The boy kept his eyes closed, and after a while he groaned from time to time. Then Mama would say, "There, there, you are going to be all right. I will make you a poultice for your wound," and he would be quiet. He closely resembled the few Indians I had seen at home, the ones who occasionally came into the city to sell fish, vegetables, and animal skins. They were said to be Mohawks, but no one really knew what their tribe was. This boy had the same features they had, the same-shaped face, and his skin was the same color, rather a nice light brown.

I was wondering what my aunt and uncle would say when we arrived with not only a pregnant niece but also a wounded

Indian when my mother, as if she had read my thoughts, suddenly smiled and said:

"Franz and Greta are good people. They will be kind to this poor young Indian."

A few minutes later Hans Grenzer raised his whip and pointed down a narrow road, at the end of which stood the farmhouse that was to be my home for an indefinite period of time. Since dusk had already fallen and the snow that had been threatening all day began to fall, I could not see the house clearly, but I remember thinking, perhaps because it was built of stone, that it looked cold and forbidding.

Chapter Four

I have searched my memory again and again, trying to put together in some kind of orderly fashion the series of events that followed our arrival at the farmhouse, but I am afraid that many of these details escape me now. One thing I do remember clearly, however, is that though the house had indeed looked uninviting at first sight, nothing could have been warmer or more welcoming than Tante Greta's greeting. After one look at Mama's tired face she drew her in through the narrow door exclaiming:

"Ach, poor tired traveler! You are weary from your trip. Come in, come in near the stove and you will feel better."

Nothing was too much trouble for her: she fed us hot soup, thick slices of bread, cheese, and stewed apples. When we had finished eating she put out large mugs of warm cider. To make us sleep, she said with a smile.

"And Franz is seeing to the Indian boy," she continued, "so you do not worry about him."

I cannot recall much more about that evening except that she took us up to a small bedroom on the second floor, where there was but one bed for Mama and me. It must have been adequate, though, because we both slept soundly.

The next day is rather a blur in my mind; it was so long ago, and though I am not feeling at my best these days I will tell you what I can. Some things stand out as plainly as if I were seeing them in a mirror, but others seem to be enveloped in a mist or haze.

I must have lain in bed late that first morning because by the time I left the cold bedroom and went down to find some breakfast in the kitchen my mother had already started for home with Hans Grenzer in that same uncomfortable wagon. At first I was hurt that she'd had no farewell for me, but later Tante Greta told me that she'd been afraid I'd cry the way I did when I was little and she left me with a neighbor while she went to the market.

"Also she worries that it might snow again," my aunt continued, handing me a bowl of apples to peel and core. "Last night's storm did not amount to more than an inch or two, but at this time of year we never know what will come next."

When I asked about the Indian boy she said he'd acted frightened, but once they had washed and bound up the gash in his arm and fed him he seemed better.

"He told me his name, Marike," she said, "something that sounds like 'Tanka,' but that may not be it. Franz took him out to the barn with him this morning. Perhaps he will do some of the work. Here, let me help you with those apples; my pastry is almost ready."

It was easy for me to settle down to life in the farmhouse, since I did almost exactly the same chores I had done for years at home. Butter and cheese had to be made, bread and cakes baked, meals prepared, and of course there was the endless cleaning and polishing that went on in all Dutch houses.

My uncle, I discovered, had bought the property some years ago from a Herr Dienstbach, a wealthy poltroon who lived in a large house several miles away, and who kept a number of servants.

"It is good living here," Tante Greta mused one evening while we sat with our knitting. "We have a nice house, a barn for the cows and horses and chickens and good land for farming, even if it is hard for Franz since the hired man went away to the army. It is a good life, Marike, and good that your Philip wants to farm."

"Hard work," commented Uncle Franz, "but that Indian boy helps. I like him and I hope he stays here. It wouldn't be the first time a young Indian in this region has left his tribe. The small-pox has wiped out many of their families. They are good workers and they seem so strong, but they lack the strength to fight off the white man's fevers. Tanka seems to be one of the best. Show him a thing one time and he knows it. He does not waste his time; when things are quiet in the barn even then he is busy. You should see the fine bow he made for himself, and the arrows! He said all the boys in his tribe had to learn how. He will kill a deer soon, and we will butcher it. That is what I understood him to say. Yes, I want him to stay."

Tanka did stay, an unobtrusive presence, all that long terrible winter. He slept in a small room, not much larger than a closet, next to the kitchen, and at first he'd take his plate of food in there to eat in spite of all my aunt's urging to sit at the table with us. He'd just shake his head and disappear.

After a couple of months, however, his shyness began to wear off and he'd sometimes spend an hour or so with us around the hearth in the kitchen. His hands were never idle: I watched with amazement at the way he fashioned a short coat for himself from the hide of a calf my uncle had slaughtered, and marveled at how quickly he made a pair of moccasins to replace the ones he'd been wearing. His English was improving, and we had no trouble understanding him when he told us that animal skins, like that of the calf, kept out the wind.

The winds were bad that year, and nowadays whenever I hear it blowing I not only remember the icy blasts and the freezing temperatures but also the worry I had concerning Philip. What news we had of the war, and it wasn't much, reached us late, so it wasn't until early March that we heard of Washington's Christmas victory at Trenton.

Yes, I said to myself, that is good news, but what of Philip? Did he survive the battle? Was he injured? What will I do if he never comes back to me? Tante Greta and Uncle Franz are wonderfully good to me, I kept reminding myself, but is this how I am to spend all my days? I find it difficult at this late date to understand the life my parents had arranged for me, but accept it I did, and without complaint. What else was I to do?

Did I lose track of time? I don't know, but the days slipped by almost unnoticed into weeks, months, and suddenly—or so it seemed to me—my daughter was two years old. She was an engaging child, and everyone loved her, especially Tanka. I remember how he delighted her with a little necklace he'd made of dried berries he'd collected in the fields and let harden. He carved small wooden toys for her, too, and when she clapped her hands and called "Ton-ton" he'd pick her up and chant a little song to her, keeping her amused while I helped Tante Greta with the cooking.

That is the kind of life I was leading when Philip unexpectedly returned.

I was in Tante Greta's vegetable patch on a bright October afternoon, piling the last of the cabbages into a wheelbarrow while Margretta played with one of the kittens, when the moment I'd been waiting for so anxiously arrived. At first I thought the man on the horse was one of the hired men coming back, and I was puzzled that he had not gone directly to the barn. I watched him dismount and come slowly toward me, limping awkwardly. Not until he called me by name did I realize who it was and that the long, long period of waiting was over. I ran to meet him, and when he took me in his arms neither of us could speak. We stood still, looking at each other, as if we knew something that needed no words.

"I went to your house on Beaver Street, Marike," Philip said when we were alone in the little bedroom that night. "Your mother was there alone. Jan and Pieter are still in the army and your father was out somewhere. At first she didn't know me; I was limping, of course, and with this scar on my face . . ."

"It will fade, my darling. You'll see," I said, staring at the angry red wound made by a Hessian's bayonet. "And then you'll forget about it."

(He never did, though, even after the wound had healed, leaving what looked like a fine seam running down the side of his face. He didn't realize that it made him look somewhat distinguished, but I did.)

"Be that as it may," he continued, "your mother did not know me, and then she was embarrassed and apologized. She made some hot milk for me—no tea or coffee is available in the city—and told me where you were and why, and what had happened to you."

"But Philip, listen to me: she doesn't know the truth. What I told her was all a lie."

"What are you saying? What?"

"I am saying the baby is yours, ours."

"How . . . I don't . . ."

"I had no chance to tell you I was with child before you went away. I wasn't really sure at that time. Then when I *was* sure, you were gone, and I didn't know what to do. You know how a baby born out of wedlock is shunned and how the mother is treated, even by her family. She's disgraced, fingers are pointed at her in the street. I knew about that; I remembered how Katje Teppich was treated. Anyway, I made up the story about the ruffians near Canvastown. It is true that they stole my money and threw me to the ground. I know they would have raped me; one of them was holding me down while the other one was pulling up my skirts, but something frightened them then, and before they could violate me they ran off. Then I thought that if I blamed the baby on them at least my family would protect me, and they did. Margretta *is* your daughter, Philip, I promise you. You must remember how we made love down by the river, don't you?"

"Yes, of course I remember, and I thought about that and you so often while I was away. But, Marike, are you sure?"

'Yes! Yes! I am sure! I am positive!" I cried. "Don't you believe me, Philip? You have but to look at her; she has your coloring, the hair, the eyes."

He said that of course he believed me, but it was some time before I could be sure that he did. The subject never came up between us again. He made a definite effort to win Margretta's affection—I think he was even a bit jealous of her love for Tanka—playing with her, telling her stories, carrying her around the orchard on his shoulders so that she could pick the apples on the lower branches, all of which delighted me.

We never heard anything about the battles he'd been in.

"I've put all that behind me, Marike," he said when I asked him about the fighting. "It would drive me mad to relive it, to talk about it. It was too terrible, too unbelievably terrible. . . ."

Chapter Five

We were married in the Dutch Reformed Church, a small stone building in the town proper of Ossining. Tanka, whose English was by this time quite fluent, told us that Ossining was an Indian name, but I forget what he said it meant. He also confirmed for us that indeed his immediate family had died of the fever that had taken many of the elders of his tribe. I never did hear what Uncle Franz told the pastor about Philip and me, but no embarrassing questions were asked, and when we left the church the little silver ring was on my finger, where it belonged.

I have wondered many times what our lives would have been like had we succumbed to Tante Greta's fervent urging to continue living with her and my uncle. Repeatedly, day after day, she pointed out the advantages of life on the farm; the plenitude of food, all the eggs, milk, butter, cheese, and fruits we could want, as well as good fresh air, which would keep us in good health.

"And just think of the pork, the bacon, the sausage," she went on. "These you will not find in a city ruled by the enemy."

It was tempting. Living with Tante Greta and Uncle Franz seemed preferable to moving in with Philip's family in New York. The baby was thriving, and Philip was looking much better than when he first arrived. He seemed anxious to help with the chores, and needless to say Uncle Franz was glad to have another pair of hands in the fields and in the barn. Tante Greta, too, was happy; I don't know how many times I heard her exclaim something like this:

"At last I have a family of my own! No longer an empty house. Now I have one filled with the sounds of young ones—oh, my, yes, this is good!"

Poor soul. She'd had bad luck with her children; two had died in infancy and a third was stillborn. It seems unfair that this should have happened to a woman who would have made such a good mother to a whole brood of children. I think, no, I am sure, that she looked forward to having us live with her (with me producing a child every year). Perhaps we would have stayed, at least through the winter, but for two separate occurrences, both of which influenced our decision to leave.

First, Philip's father died suddenly, and my husband was needed to take over the chandlery. Second, the British, who at that time were in control of both sides of the Hudson, ran short of supplies and began to send groups of soldiers out to raid the barns and cellars of the farmers in our area, terrifying everyone, including ourselves.

Tante Greta was showing me how to make a pudding using dried corn and telling me with pride that there were enough ears stashed away to last until next summer when the new crop would be ready.

"And think, Marike," she was saying, smiling as she spoke, "think of the apples we have, the turnips, the sauerkraut I'll make; we'll live like kings!"

Perhaps we would have lived well, but I'll never know because almost before she finished speaking sudden shouts and loud noises out in the yard shattered the peace of that warm kitchen, startling us both and causing Margretta to whimper. From the window we saw two British soldiers running toward the barn while two more approached the house.

"Hide, Marike, hide!" my aunt cried, picking Margretta up and starting for the stairs. "They will kill us all!"

Panic-stricken, I ran to bolt the heavy back door, and turning, picked up the heaviest kitchen utensil I could see, a cast-iron skillet with a fairly long wooden handle. I thought I could swing it at the head of anyone breaking into the house. Then I remembered how the two ruffians near Canvastown had knocked me down, and I wondered if the soldiers would do the same.

A loud cry, an unmistakable howl of pain, caused me to hurry back to the window. At first I saw only that one of the soldiers had turned and, instead of coming to the house, was now running hard toward the shelter of the trees at the edge of the property. A moment later I spotted the second man. He was lying motionless on the ground with an arrow sticking out of his back.

"You can thank the good Lord he sent Tanka into our path, Marike," Uncle Franz said later that afternoon. "He is a hero, no doubt about it. Even if the soldiers hadn't killed us, and they might have, they'd have taken everything and we'd have starved to death. That boy is remarkable, remarkable. When he saw the two coming into the barn he threw the rope he was coiling around the neck of the first one and choked him to death. And then there's Philip, ah, he knows how to fight; he flung a hatchet at the other's head, knocked him insensible. Later, Tanka shot the arrow you saw, and finished off the other two. A hero, that's what that boy is. And your Philip, too, Marike."

"The bodies, Franz, what do we do with them? The British . . ." Tante Greta, looking pale and worried, clutched her husband's arm. "The British," she repeated hoarsely. "Will they come for them? Will they come for us?"

"No, no, my Greta," he answered, patting her hand, "The British are far too occupied with the war, and besides, Tanka and Philip are just now burying the three men. They will never be found, thanks to Tanka's skill."

"They will come for us," my aunt said nervously, clasping and unclasping her hands. "We are no longer safe here. Why did they have to kill them? He could have given them food and they would have gone away and left us in peace."

"Let them take our livestock and set fire to the barn?" Uncle Franz asked angrily. "Never! Never!"

The argument went on, long after Philip and Tanka came in to sit exhaustedly by the stove. I could see how miserable my aunt was—we all were, come to think of it—and I dreaded making her even more unhappy by telling her that I had made up my mind to return to the city to live with Philip's family. I waited almost a week before I spoke.

"We have no choice, Tante Greta," I said one morning after

the men had gone outside. "Philip is needed to take over his father's business. His mother and sisters have no other means of support. God only knows when Philip will have the farm he has set his heart on now. I don't want to go, but what else can I do? I am his wife."

In the end she agreed that we were doing the right thing, and after making me promise to return whenever I could, she set about helping me pack our few possessions as well as boxes of foodstuffs she was sure we would never find in the city.

A few days later we left. My last glimpse of that good woman as we started out in the wagon that Uncle Franz and Tanka had helped Philip repair is unforgettable. She was standing in the doorway waving to us as the wind whipped her full skirts about her ankles. She tried to smile, but I could see tears slipping slowly down over her soft, plump cheeks.

Chapter Six

D
o not worry if we are stopped by soldiers when we come near the city, Marike," Philip said after we had been traveling for several hours. "I heard from a fellow who stopped by the farm the other day on his way to Albany that they are looking for troublemakers. Apparently there are gangs, one is called the Levellers, who attack the Loyalists. We look harmless enough, a not too well-off family, which I guess we are, and if they ask why we wish to enter the city we can say that my mother is sick and needs help, which is near enough to the truth."

As it happened, we came across no soldiers or guards of any kind. We did see a small building, no bigger than a hut, at the side of the road, which Philip said was probably one of their posts.

"Will they come out and stop us?" I asked nervously.

"No," he answered. "I don't think so. It looks deserted. Perhaps the guards were needed in the city, or maybe they went off to a tavern to get warm. Nothing is colder than guard duty. I know."

It can't be much colder than riding in an open wagon on a day like this, I thought as I adjusted the blankets I'd wrapped around Margretta and myself and then tried to take my mind off the discomfort of this seemingly endless trip.

Over the years I have forgotten many things and contrariwise have remembered unimportant trifles, like the fact that it was the thirteenth day of November in the year 1779 when I had my first glimpse of the city in more than two years. Perhaps I remember it because the place looked so awful that I nearly asked Philip to turn around and go back to Ossining. The sight that met my eyes reminded me of the devastation after the fire of 1776, of ruined houses and tumbledown shacks. I heard later that General Washington, who viewed the city from across the Hudson at about that time, stated in a report that he was startled by the emptiness he saw, the lack of trees and houses. Philip said the British had probably burned everything for firewood.

It wasn't so much the lack of trees that shocked me; outlying farms had an abandoned look, and once well-kept houses owned by prosperous merchants stood forlorn and empty, with broken windows, sagging doors, and no sign of life.

"The British," Philip muttered as he urged the horse onward. "The damned British. It gets worse and worse. . . ."

"Shouldn't we turn back?" I asked finally, thinking of the comfort and warmth of the farmhouse.

"No, Marike," he said shortly. "We can't do that. My place is here, and your place is with me now. Also, you will want to see your own family, won't you?"

When I didn't respond immediately he looked at me, and seeing my troubled expression he put an arm around my shoulders.

"Don't worry, my love," he said more gently. "We must make the best of things now, and later on we'll have our own place, our own farm, I promise you."

Most of the details of our arrival at the Bogardus home escape me now—I was bone-weary at the time—but I know that somehow the wagon was unloaded, the horse stabled, and we were at last indoors. It is probably always difficult for a young woman to move into the household of her husband's mother, and my own experience was neither pleasant nor memorable. I felt unwelcome from the moment I stepped into the three-story house on Water Street until the day I left it. Mrs. Bogardus hardly glanced at Margretta and me when Philip introduced us before launching into a complaint (I was to learn she was a chronic complainer) about Essie, the slave girl, who had run away to work for the British.

"They promised her freedom, Philip," she cried, "and money. Whoever heard of paying a slave? And who is to do the cooking? The cleaning? The washing?"

"We will help you, Mama," Philip said quietly, "and I will try to find someone—"

"Who is there to find?" she interrupted. "They've all gone away, all the good ones who did housework, gone God knows where! There is no one to be had, no one!" With that she turned away from us, pulling a heavy shawl more closely around her thin body.

47

All this time we'd been standing just inside the front door. I thought that at any moment I might collapse from weariness and hunger, but fortunately Philip's two sisters came running down the stairs just then and took charge of the situation. Anna, the older one, put an arm around her mother, and murmuring words of consolation led her into the front room, established her in an armchair, and wrapped yet another shawl around her. Louisa, younger and prettier than her sister, called out from halfway down the hall that she would return and greet us properly as soon as she brought the potion for her mother.

I had no idea what the potion was meant to cure, but it did have a calming effect on Mrs. Bogardus, who sat quite still, paying attention only to Philip as she recounted the long list of hardships she was forced to endure. Then, suddenly, without any warning, she sat up straight and pointed an accusing finger at me where I stood holding Margretta in my arms.

"That ring!" she exclaimed. "That ring belongs to me! Why are you wearing my ring? Give it here at once!"

"Oh, Mama," Philip said wearily, "don't you remember? Grossmoeder gave me the ring to give to my wife."

"Nonsense!" she cried. "It was meant for me. It is mine by right."

"No, Mama, it is Marike's. You know it was given to me."

I set Margretta down close to me and began to slide the little silver ring from my finger, but Philip shook his head at me and pointed to the door. Anna, seeing that I looked puzzled, whispered: "Come with me," and after handing me an oil lamp she gathered Margretta into her arms and led the way out of the room and up the stairs.

Chapter Seven

I t's best to keep out of Mama's way when she takes one of her spells," Anna murmured when we reached the third floor. "That's why Louisa and I were not downstairs when you came; she'd been carrying on about Essie until we were nearly crazy."

"Does this happen often?" I asked.

"It didn't used to, but lately, ever since Papa died, it's worse. Look, here's your room. It was Philip's until he went away, and we've kept it just as he left it. And here, this smaller one next to it will do nicely for the baby. There's another little room in the back, the one that Essie had. She kept it clean, and after she left Louisa and I gave it a good turning out." She set Margretta on the bed.

"Brr-r! It's cold up here. You'll need to bring up some warm bricks to put in the beds, but don't let Mama see you do it. She's afraid we'll run out of coal, but Papa, bless him, left a big supply of it in the cellar. Don't even mention that to anyone, anyone at all, because if the British got wind of it they'd be after it in a minute."

While she was speaking, I looked around my husband's boyhood room, noting the neatly made-up bed our daughter now sat on, the oval braided rug next to it, the hooks on the wall for clothing, and the single straight-backed chair. Little attention had been lavished on the furnishings or on those of the smaller room next to it, which contained only a narrow cot and a ramshackle three-drawer chest. If only it weren't so cold, I thought, if only . . .

Footsteps sounded on the stairs, and moments later Philip staggered in with our boxes. He looked as tired as I felt, but he managed a small smile when Anna said what we all needed was some hot food and a night's sleep. She made that sound so comforting that I felt like hugging her.

There was not much that was comforting about the house itself, though, partly because it was so cold and also because it was dark. The windows, as in most Dutch houses, were small, meant to keep out the cold, but they also restricted the light.

It was a tall, narrow house. The front room and the kitchen, which took up all the space on the ground floor, were fairly large, although the former was so filled with chairs, tables, and cabinets that it never seemed spacious. I didn't like it. The kitchen was more cheerful with its scrubbed pine table in the center and the old but comfortable rocking chair next to the huge coal range. The three bedrooms on the second floor, one for Mrs. Bogardus and two smaller ones for Anna and Louisa, were sparsely furnished, but adequate. To my mind my mother's house had much more to recommend it as far as comfort was concerned.

I do not know if it is true that the winter of 1780 was the worst one ever in New York, but I do know that the bitter cold kept us indoors for days on end, and that even inside the house it was a struggle to stay warm. The Hudson River froze completely over, and Philip told us that he'd seen men driving cattle and teams of horses across the unusually thick ice on the East River.

There was, as Anna had said, a good supply of coal in the cellar, but Mrs. Bogardus complained every time she saw one of us bringing up a small sack for the grate in the front room or the kitchen range. What didn't she complain about? The food was either raw or overcooked, the floors were never properly cleaned, her potion was not warm, and she had no sugar for her porridge. It was of no use to tell her that no one had any sugar for anything. Food was scarce throughout the city, and once the supplies Tante Greta had packed for us were gone we ate poorly.

Philip, who went daily to the chandlery, would occasionally bring home a small bag of flour or cornmeal he had taken in payment from a British supply officer who was short of money, but it never lasted long. We were always hungry, and if it hadn't been for the potatoes, carrots, and turnips stored in the root cellar I don't know what we would have done.

"If you think we're badly off," Philip said one night when we were making a meal of hot potato soup, "listen to this: a man came into the shop today, but not to buy anything—he just wanted to get out of the cold for a few minutes. We talked, and after a while he read me a letter he'd had from a cousin who'd been taken prisoner by the British in the battle out on Long Island. The man—the cousin, I mean—managed to smuggle the letter out from one of the prison ships in Wallabout Bay. Conditions there are worse than anythig I ever heard of; most of the prisoners' clothes have been confiscated, and they're freezing to death. He wrote that the food is nothing but scraps, rotten scraps, and up to a dozen men die every day of the pox or yellow fever."

"Oh, oh, my son," Mrs. Bogardus cried, "they will come for you, take you prisoner! What will we do then? The little money you bring in will be gone. Oh, oh," she wailed. "And now we have two more mouths to feed besides ourselves, your wife and her bastard! No, no, do not look at me like that. I know."

"Mama! Mama!" Philip shouted. "That is not true . . ."

"It is! It is!" she shrieked, banging her hands on the table. "Why else was she sent away to have the baby?"

"Enough!" Philip's voice was angry, almost a growl. "Enough, Mama. She is my child, and if I ever hear you say one more word to the contrary I'll take Marike and Margretta away and leave you."

"Oh, no, no," she sobbed. "Louisa, my potion . . ."

"What is in that potion your mother takes?" I asked Anna the next morning when we were clearing up in the kitchen. She smiled slightly, and putting a finger to her lips motioned to me to follow her up the stairs.

"She has sharper ears than you would think," she said quietly, seating herself at the end of my bed and handing Margretta her little rag doll. "But she can't hear me now. For a long time I didn't know what was in the potion. For a while it was something called 'Gideon's Cordial.' You've seen that old bottle on the shelf, haven't you?"

I nodded, and after a moment or two she continued: "It came from England. Papa brought it home, and it seemed to calm her down. She didn't take much of it, hardly any until after he died, and when it was all gone she went frantic."

"I wanted to send for a doctor, but she wouldn't have one. She said all they did for people was to bleed them, or purge them, or make them vomit. Then she told me to take the empty bottle to the widow Riddell and ask her to fill it. So, I went, not willingly, but I went. I had no choice. I don't like the widow; she frightens me with her small black eyes and her strange, whispery voice. She lives in a messy little house near Collect Pond, and has bunches of dried flowers and herbs—they look like weeds to me—hanging all over the place. Anyway, when I showed her the bottle and the money Mama gave me she got busy, saying she needed to pound willow bark and yarrow and wormwood. She did this, and when she had a fine powder she put it in my bottle and then filled it up with some kind of liquid.

"I asked her if that was water, and she sort of cackled and said 'Water! Hoo! Hoo! No, child, that's rum, genuine rum, just like what was in this old bottle.'

"Then, she asked me to bring a larger bottle next time, so now we use the big one in the cupboard under the stairs. I'll have to go again soon." Anna sighed as she rose from the bed and started for the door. "The bottle is more than half empty. Oh, I do hate going there. I wish Louisa would do it, but she won't." She paused and looked toward the door. "Well, I'd better get on downstairs now. Mama will be wondering where I am and what I'm doing."

After she left, I sat watching Margretta play with the little doll, going over in my mind what Anna had said. Louisa should go, I thought; she seemed to enjoy her role as preparer of the potion, and she also seemed to like the taste of it. I knew that, because on two separate occasions I had seen her take a surreptitious sip or two from the pewter cup before presenting it to her mother.

Louisa was a quiet, unobtrusive girl, quick to do whatever chores were assigned to her and, when they were done, to sit for long periods of time staring, rather vacantly, I thought, at nothing in particular. Philip told me she had been slow to speak as a child and that he thought it was a good thing she was pretty because she wasn't very smart.

"Philip, perhaps we should live in my father's house," I said when we were getting ready for bed the night after his mother's latest outburst. "My old room is empty, and the boys are away—"

"Wait, dearest, wait a little. My mother will be afraid to say anything like that again," he said, taking me in his arms. "She knows I made no idle threat. I will take you and my daughter away, I promise, if she does."

Strangely enough it took his mother's accusation to convince me that he really believed Margretta to be his child. In a way I was grateful to her, for then I knew beyond any doubt that he had discarded what he'd heard from my own mother and that he believed me. That is all that matters, Marike, I said to myself, that Philip believes you.

Would we have been better off in my parents' house on Beaver Street? I've often wondered. Possibly not, judging from the way my mother acted on the few occasions I'd been to see her. I took Margretta with me, and each time I came away with the feeling that the visit had not been entirely successful.

Try as I might, I could not find the right moment or the correct words to tell Mama the truth about her grandchild, or perhaps I lacked the courage to do so. Then, of course, there'd be my father to face, not at all a pleasant prospect. Stay where you are, I said to myself. You can deal better with Mrs. Bogardus than you can with your own parents; a sad state of affairs when all is said and done.

Anna and Louisa did their best to shield me from their mother's faultfinding and complaining during the daytime, and when Philip was home in the evening the old lady was careful to leave me alone. Once she even smiled at me across the supper table, or so I thought at the time. Later I decided she'd been smiling to herself at the thought of what she was planning to do when the opportunity arose.

I should have been suspicious, should have wondered about the subtle change in her manner toward me, but I was too pleased (or too stupid) to see any ulterior motive in her sudden display of concern for my welfare.

"Do you need an extra featherbed to keep you warm, my dear?" she asked me one especially cold afternoon when I was sitting close to the kitchen range while Margretta amused herself with a bag of clothes pegs at the table.

When I thanked her and said that Philip and I were warm enough at night a strange expression crossed her face, a sort of sneer, but moments later she smiled and said she thought Margretta was becoming quite pretty. She was indeed an engaging child, with Philip's blue, blue eyes and curly blond hair. Why, I wondered suddenly, didn't my own mother suspect the truth when she looked at Margretta? Perhaps she did, and preferred to say nothing.

"Something to drink, Marike?" Mrs. Bogardus asked a few nights later. "Something to help you sleep soundly? You are looking pale, and with a good night's rest you will be able to keep up your strength."

"Thank you, thank you very much," I replied, "but I am so tired at the end of the day that I fall asleep as soon as I am in bed."

I thought no more of those conversations for several days, maybe a week or more. Then I caught a chill, which left me with an annoying cough. Philip was concerned, and I knew why: people throughout the city were dying not only of cold and starvation, but also of all manner of fevers and chest ailments for which there were no known cures.

"I'll try to find some lemons, dearest," he said one evening after noticing that I had trouble swallowing the mashed turnips and potatoes at supper. "Mama, isn't there some of Papa's whiskey left? A spoonful of that mixed with lemon juice and hot water would ease Marike's throat."

"In the cupboard under the stairs," she answered, "but you could just as well use some of the peach brandy your father liked so much."

I did not want to drink either whiskey or peach brandy, but after I had tucked Margretta into her bed that night, Philip came upstairs and handed me a mug filled with a sweet-smelling, steaming liquid.

"Drink it after you are in bed," he said. "It will stop the coughing long enough for you to get to sleep. I'll stay here to make sure you're all right and that Margretta is off for the night. Then I'll go down and bring up some coal for the stove. Anna says that if I do it tonight Mama won't make a fuss."

"Poor Philip," I said, thinking how unpleasant my hoarse voice must sound to him. "Poor man, working so hard all day and coming home to a sick wife and . . ."

"A difficult mother," he finished with a wry grin, "to put it mildly. It's not so bad, though. The chandlery's a good place to work in. You'll have to pay me a visit there when you're better, and bring Margretta with you. I'll find some bits and pieces for her to play with."

Three days later my cough had improved to the point where I thought I could do without any more of the precious peach brandy, but when Philip sent word by Adam, his young errand boy, that he would be late coming home (a ship due to sail on the morning tide needed outfitting) Mrs. Bogardus said she would make up a hot drink for me herself.

"Oh, you must have it," she said quickly when I protested that I no longer needed it. "A good sleep is the best thing for you. See how much better you are today. Go up now, my dear. Put the child to bed, and I will send Louisa up with the brandy and hot water."

There was no arguing with her, so I simply thanked her and said good night. I knew what I was going to do, though, and when Louisa appeared with the mug I asked her to put it down, saying I would drink it later on. Whether it was because I had not liked the deep sleep the brandy had induced the previous nights or whether I was suspicious of the old lady's motive I do not know, but I could no more have swallowed the mixture she'd prepared than I could have flown out the window.

There was no place I could pour the liquid away without going downstairs again, so I pushed the mug under the bed, thinking I'd get rid of it in the morning, and prepared myself for sleep. The moon must have been full, or nearly full, that night because it shone through our one small window, lighting up a section of the wall opposite the bed, a comfort to me in Philip's absence.

I fell asleep before he came in, but some time later—it couldn't have been much later—something woke me up. The pattern made by the moonlight had shifted slightly and I turned over, tucking my right hand under my cheek in order to see it better. I never did like being alone in the dark, and I remember hoping I'd be sound asleep before the moonlight disappeared. I must have slept, or I would have heard her coming. I was dreaming that one of my hands was caught in a tangle of ropes or wires when I woke up and felt something or someone trying to ease the silver ring from the fourth finger of my left hand.

I screamed, and probably would have gone on screaming if Philip hadn't appeared in the doorway holding an oil lamp and asking what was the matter. His mother turned away from the side of the bed, and murmuring something about coming in to see how I was, she hurried from the room.

"She thought she was going to take the ring," I sobbed while Philip held me in his arms. "Then she'd say I lost it. She thought I'd drunk the brandy she sent up with Louisa and would be in a deep sleep, and you weren't here . . ."

"Don't cry, my love; I'm here now, and I'll see to it that she never tries anything like that again," he said, patting my shoulder and kissing me gently.

"If I'd had the brandy—as she thought I had—oh, she was insistent that I have it even though I said I didn't need it. She would have taken the ring. She had it halfway off my finger."

"Yes," he said, thoughtfully, "she would have taken it and probably hidden it away."

"Should we give it to her, Philip? Would that—"

"No, absolutely not. My grandmother, my father's mother, did not want her to have it. She said my father had been generous enough to her. Anyway, she has a ring of her own. Haven't you seen it? It's gold, and far more valuable than this one. I can't understand why she wants yours, but then I've never understood lots of things about her. Not even what my father saw in her."

"Maybe she was different when she was young," I said, pulling his head down so that I could kiss him. "Come now, come to bed. We must get some sleep."

To my surprise Mrs. Bogardus was perfectly affable when we met in the kitchen the next morning. She said nothing about the previous night, nor did she protest or offer any suggestions when I announced that I was going to take Margretta to see the chandler's shop in the early afternoon.

"Oh, it will do you good to get out, Marike," Anna said, nodding her head so vigorously that one of her combs bounced out. "It's still cold, but if you walk in the sunshine it will not be too bad."

"And see if Philip has come across any sugar," her mother

added. "And tea. How I long for a cup of good tea with sugar in it! It would be good for you, too, Marike."

I nodded, but said nothing. I was still somewhat shaken by the events of the previous night, but not so upset that I failed to see a pattern starting to repeat itself: pretended interest in my health to put me off my guard. That's exactly what it was, and she did it so well that it could easily pass for genuine concern. While I vowed silently that I would not be fooled again I smiled pleasantly as I wondered what she'd do next. I soon found out.

When we entered the chandlery later that day I felt as if I were stepping into a foreign land, not a large one to be sure, but one filled with objects I had never seen before. Shelves filled with lanterns of all sizes and shapes lined one wall, while all sorts of supplies for sea voyages were displayed around the shop. Barrels of ropes, along with various sizes of anchors, took up most of the floor space, and boxes containing sextants and other instruments were piled carefully against another wall. I particularly liked the look of the neat rows of drawers with brass handles that occupied the space behind the counter in the rear of the store.

"Everything a ship needs," Adam, the errand boy, said proudly as I looked around. "See over here, ma'am, we have extra canvas. Needles are kept in that drawer. And we have boots and oilskins, even quill pens and ink for the logs and record books."

"Isn't it hard to come by these things with the war going on and everyone so badly off?" I asked.

"That it is, ma'am," he answered, "but Philip's pa knew a lot of people, and since he never caused the British any trouble they let him deal where he wanted to. He stored up much stuff—you should see what's in the back room and in the loft. And now they treat Philip the same way, even though they know he fought against them. It's because they *need* all these things, couldn't sail without them."

One of the things I liked best about the chandlery was the pleasant smell of the place. Philip told me it came from the oil and wood tar that was used to keep the ropes and fishing lines in workable condition. Whatever it was, it was a relief from the dusty, dead air in the house on Water Street, with its tightly closed windows. Maybe the fresh air that blew into the shop with the ships' supply officers helped.

These men and the occasional sailor (all British, of course), coming in for various articles, showed no surprise at the sight of a woman perched on a three-legged stool and a small child playing on the floor with little blocks of wood. Their minds were so taken up with their purchases that we might not have been there at all. Philip and Adam were both kept busy for some time, but after a while when Adam had followed the last customer out, carrying a heavy box of supplies, Philip came over to where I sat and held a small object out to me.

"This will enable you to sleep nights when I'm late coming in," he said softly. "It's a special latch that I will fasten to the bedroom door. It's no use saying anything to my mother; she'd just deny everything—I learned that years ago—but this will keep her out. You're a light sleeper, you hear the slightest sound Margretta makes, so when I come in I'll knock softly like this." He tapped twice slowly on the wall behind me and then three times quickly. "Then you'll know who it is."

"Do Anna and Louisa know what happened?" I asked after a moment or two.

"I don't think so," he answered. "But I can't be sure. They'd be horrified, but not surprised. They're used to her and put up with her, but they'll both get out of there as soon as they can. Anna's in love; he's in the British army, seems like a nice fellow, and I hope he comes back. And Louisa, well, I don't know."

"She's so pretty," I said. "She's sure to marry once the war is over."

"Maybe, but right now she's under my mother's thumb."

"I'm afraid I'll never trust your mother, Philip," I said, taking Margretta onto my lap.

"Neither will I," he said quickly. "And I'll get us out of there as soon as I can afford to. I've started making some investments, small ones for now, but they'll bring in some money. I go over to the counting house now and then and buy shares in ships traveling up and down the coast, and some investments have paid off pretty well. When the war is over that trade is bound to increase, and then we'll have plenty of money."

The door to the chandlery suddenly burst open and Adam rushed in, but before he could say anything Margretta slid from my lap and ran to the arms of the man following the errand boy, crying "Ton-Ton" and laughing delightedly. I heard Adam say, "He followed me . . ." but the rest was lost in the welcome that Philip and I (and of course, Margretta) gave the tall, young Indian.

Chapter Eight

T anka's arrival caused no stir of excitement on the streets of New York, where the inhabitants were accustomed to seeing the Indians who came in from outlying regions to sell whatever food and furs they could, but the uproar he caused in the house on Water Street when Philip brought him home was another matter.

"What's this? An Indian! A red Indian!" screamed Mrs. Bogardus when Tanka came into the kitchen holding Margretta by the hand. "Out! Get out of my house at once!"

"Mama, wait! Listen to me!" Philip cried, taking hold of his mother's arm. "Tanka is a friend. He saved our lives."

"Friend, nothing! He will kill us all!"

"I go. Is better I go," Tanka said, starting for the door.

"No go, Ton-Ton," pleaded Margretta, beginning to cry, "No go."

How long the argument between Philip and his mother went on I don't remember, but some time later that evening after Louisa had administered not one but two doses of the potion,

Mrs. Bogardus quieted down and allowed her daughters to help her up the stairs and into bed.

"Mama will not be down for supper," Anna said as we sat down to a meal of chopped carrots and turnips that had been simmering on the coal range until it was almost tasteless. "But tell us, Tanka, what brings you to New York?"

Slowly and quietly he told us that since the British were no longer in the Ossining area and there was not much for him to do at the farm in the winter months, Uncle Franz had sent him to us, thinking our need for protection was greater than his and my aunt's.

"I help in the shop? I work?" he asked, looking at Philip, who nodded and said we must find a place for Tanka to sleep.

"He could have the little room on your floor, Philip," Anna said. "Essie's old room. There's only a cot in there, but tomorrow I'll see what I can do."

"I'll help you, Anna," the usually quiet Louisa said. "He can have that extra chair . . ." She broke off, as if embarrassed, and looked down at her plate. She seemed fascinated by Tanka, hardly taking her eyes off him, and smiling happily whenever he turned to look at her.

"Yes," Anna went on. "We will make him as comfortable as we can."

As things turned out the two sisters didn't have to do anything for Tanka's comfort. When their mother realized that "the red Indian" had slept in her house she went into such a tantrum, screaming, throwing things around, and threatening to kill herself, that Tanka fled, saying he'd sleep in the back room at the shop. I was surprised he didn't go straight back to the farm and

Tante Greta's good meals. But, of course, Tanka stayed because he knew he was needed.

As Philip said, I am a light sleeper, and several times during the nights that followed Tanka's arrival I was awakened by creaking sounds on the stairs that could only have been made by someone going stealthily up or down. I knew without a doubt that it was Mrs. Bogardus. Was she coming up to see if we had secreted Tanka in the little bedroom, or had she something else in mind? I never found out.

I didn't tell Philip about those sounds; he slept soundly and was never aware of them. Nor did I mention that I suspected his mother of wandering around in the dark. I couldn't add to his burdens; he worked too hard and had enough on his mind without having to listen to the chatter of a nervous wife.

After a while what I had come to call "the night noises" ceased, or perhaps I no longer heard them. In any case I was sleeping better and feeling well physically in spite of being in the house so much on account of the weather. The winter seemed to last and last, and just when we thought the snow was over a big storm, really a blizzard, covered the city with several feet of new snow, bringing misery to its war- and winter-weary inhabitants.

Late one afternoon, Margretta and I were in the kitchen with Anna and Louisa listening to the howling wind and watching the snow being blown almost horizontally and piled up into huge drifts when Philip and Tanka staggered in through the back door.

"Don't worry, Tanka," Anna said quietly, seeing Tanka's anxious expression as he looked around the room. "Mama's gone to bed. She had a bad headache."

"I couldn't leave him in the shop," Philip interrupted. "Snow was coming in—the roof needs fixing—we'll get to it tomorrow. We covered the supplies with sailcloth so they'll be all right, but Tanka would have frozen to death in there tonight."

We were unusually cheerful that night, sitting in a semicircle around the big stove while the storm raged outside. Philip told us stories about some of his strange customers and made us laugh. There was one he told about two French sailors who mistook the chandlery for a store selling ladies' nightgowns. Louisa surprised me again: as usual, she didn't say much, but instead of staring vacantly into space she kept her eyes on Tanka's face as he sat with Margretta on his lap, trying to get her to repeat the words of a little Indian song.

The meal itself, consisting as it did of the everlasting potato, carrot, and turnip soup, was by no means special, but it was filling and I kept telling myself that we were lucky to have even that. I didn't go to bed hungry, but my last thoughts that night before falling asleep were of my mother's oilcakes and buttermilk biscuits and of Tante Greta's puddings and spicy apple tarts. I could almost smell the nutmeg in the pudding and the cinnamon of the apple tarts.

A loud bang, like that made when a door slams, woke Philip and me up while it was still dark. I lighted the oil lamp and listened for Margretta, but she was quiet.

"The wind is—" Whatever Philip was going to say was cut off by a scream, followed by a horrible, crazy kind of laughter in the hall outside our bedroom. I picked up the oil lamp and caught up with Philip at the top of the stairs, just in time to see two figures reach the floor below before the flickering light of the candle one of them held was blown out.

"That was Louisa, and my mother was with her," Philip whispered. "What on earth?"

"Louisa was probably trying to get your mother back to bed. . . . Oh, Tanka! What happened?" I asked as the Indian appeared beside me.

"The door make noise: *Bang!* I see light," he answered. "Someone cry out."

"She could have set the house on fire with that candle," Philip said with a groan. "I don't know what she'll do next. And I don't know what I should do. I can't put her out in the street. God help me! Tell me what to do!"

We finally went back to bed. Miraculously, Margretta had slept through all the noise, and Philip and I managed a few hours of sleep before a cold dawn broke over the snow-covered city.

Chapter Nine

By morning the storm was over, but the bitter cold that so often follows a heavy snow settled over New York like a blanket of ice. Both Margretta and Louisa looked nervously around for Tanka when we gathered in the kitchen, but he had evidently slipped out before the rest of us were awake. Philip said he was probably anxious to get started on the repairing of the roof over the back room at the chandlery, but I knew he was trying to avoid more unpleasantness.

"He's happiest when he's working, when he's busy," Philip continued. "Remember, Marike, how your uncle said what a good worker—"

He broke off abruptly when his mother appeared in the doorway and from the way he looked at her, I knew he was wondering how much of the previous night's incident she remembered. She looked pale and only toyed with the bowl of cornmeal mush Anna put in front of her, but she said nothing. Except for Margretta's chatter the meal was for the most part a silent one, not at all a promising start to the day.

After Philip left, Mrs. Bogardus went into the front room and sat down close to the coal fire, as was her habit, with an old leather-bound copy of Calvin's sermons on her lap. She may have read some of them, but I rather think the book was merely meant to signify that she was a good, pious woman, since I never saw her turn a page.

"Another day in this dreary house," Anna sighed. "Nothing to do but the cleaning and scrubbing. I think I'd even relish a trip to the widow's, just to get out. Put that broom down, Marike; sit here at the table and talk to me. Oh, I'm so tired; that ruckus last night woke me up, and then Louisa cried for hours. How did Mama know Tanka was here, anyway?"

"According to Philip she may not have known," I answered. "He thinks she heard Louisa going up to the third floor and followed her. She could have seen Tanka when Louisa opened the door to that room. Then one of them slammed the door and your mother dragged Louisa down the stairs. That's what Philip thinks."

"Louisa was crazy to do a thing like that," Anna said slowly. "She has no sense at all. I don't know what will become of her. I'll probably have to take care of her for the rest of my life, and I have my own plans—for after the war. She's fallen in love with him, hasn't she, Marike?"

When I nodded in assent she sighed and said bitterly: "If he married her she'd be off my hands, but I don't suppose I'll be that lucky. Sometimes I think I hate her as much as I hate my mother."

"Anna, Anna," Mrs. Bogardus called, her raspy voice making

us both jump. "Bring me another shawl. Do you want me to perish with the cold?"

"Yes," Anna muttered under her breath as she pushed her chair back and got wearily to her feet: "I'm sick and tired of waiting on you. I'm not a servant. . . ."

There was never the slightest chance that Tanka would marry poor Louisa; her mother saw to that. Try as I might, I can't forget what that wretched woman did, and I'm pretty sure I can give an accurate description of what happened:

A few days after my conversation with Anna the weather became warmer, and I was able to take Margretta out for a short time in the afternoons. On this particular day we had just returned from visiting my mother and were no sooner inside the house when we heard raised voices in the front room. I paused in the doorway, uncertain whether to go in or not, and listened.

Mrs. Bogardus was shouting something about Indians, Anna was saying "Mama, stop it, stop!" and Louisa was crying. When the old lady caught sight of me she turned away from her daughters. She'd found a new target for her wrath.

"It is all your fault, you miserable, sinful girl," she said in a low, menacing voice that was more frightening than all her shouting and screaming. "You brought that Indian here. Yes, it is your fault. Now Louisa is mad for him; I found her today up in the room he had slept in, lying on the bed he defiled. She is mad, mad, and you, you . . ."

"Mama, mama, come sit down, sit down again," Anna pleaded, trying to take her mother's arm.

"No, no! Go away!" cried Mrs. Bogardus, pushing Anna aside

and picking up the cane she occasionally used. "Louisa has sinned. She had done something evil and must be punished, yes, punished! That Indian is bad!"

At this point Louisa, who had been moaning as she rocked back and forth on her knees in front of the fire, burst into loud sobs.

"Tanka is good," she gasped when she could speak. "Good, good."

"Ah, hear what she says! She sins! Still she sins!" cried her mother. "Louisa, stop that rocking! Stay still. Take your beating!"

I started to move forward, thinking I might somehow protect the young girl, but Mrs. Bogardus, showing more strength than I would have thought possible, pushed me away so forcefully that I fell against the round table that stood in the middle of the room, knocking it over and breaking the large delft bowl we had all been forbidden to touch. For a few moments there was silence in the room, but by the time I had struggled back to the doorway and taken Margretta into my arms, I heard Anna again remonstrating.

"Mama, Mama, don't," she cried, lunging forward and seizing the cane her mother was about to bring down on the back of the miserable girl crouching on the hearth rug. She tossed it to one side, and then, grasping the old lady around the waist, forced her into the big armchair. Mrs. Bogardus let her head sink down onto her chest and began to rock back and forth much as her younger daughter had done. Strange, whimpering sounds came from her for a few moments; then suddenly she sat up straight and demanded her potion.

"No more potions today, Mama," Anna said firmly. "You've had enough of it."

"Bring it!" her mother commanded. "I said bring it!"

Anna sighed and left the room, picking up the cane as she went and taking it with her. I waited until she returned with a cup of the steaming liquid, and after a last glance at the softly moaning Louisa, I took Margretta up to the quiet of the third floor.

"Your wife broke my delft bowl, Philip," Mrs. Bogardus said while we were finishing our meal that night. "I treasured that bowl. Your papa gave it to me a long time ago."

"Yes, but you pushed Marike so hard that she fell against the table," he answered. (He'd heard the entire story from Anna and me earlier.) "Have you finished eating, Mama? he asked, staring at her intently. "If so, please come into the front room with me."

Puzzled, she looked at him for a moment before nodding and getting up from the table.

"He's the only one who can do anything with her," Anna said once we heard the closing of a door. "She's afraid he'll leave and that there'll be no one to run the chandlery and bring in the money."

"Tanka could," Louisa said softly.

"Don't ever say that!" Anna exclaimed. "And don't ever mention his name in front of Mama. You almost got a beating today for mooning over him. She was so angry I thought she was going to kill you."

"I know, I know. I won't, I won't," her sister promised. "But I have to think about him."

"It would be better if you didn't think about him, Louisa," I said gently, but I doubt that she heard me. We talked on quietly for some time, but since Philip did not return to the kitchen and the door to the front room remained closed, I took a sleepy Margretta up to bed and waited for him in our room.

Louisa kept her promise, and life in the Bogardus house was relatively peaceful—I cannot say it was pleasant—for the six or eight weeks following the dreadful scene in the front room. Anna said she thought Philip had laid down the law to his mother, for she not only stopped complaining about trifles but also began to help with some of the easier chores, dusting the furniture, peeling the potatoes, things like that. She even walked over to the widow Riddell's house one fine afternoon to replenish the supply of her potion.

The spring of 1780 was not, however, a happy time in my parents' home on Beaver Street; word came that both my brothers had been killed in the fighting at Saratoga. My mother was distraught, my father dispirited; there was nothing I could do or say to comfort either one of them, and I would come away from their house feeling not only sad but also useless. It was with relief, a relief tinged with guilt, that I'd turn my attention to Margretta's happy little face and say yes, we'll stop in at the chandlery and see Tanka.

One day in particular stands out in my memory, a lovely afternoon in April when the air was fresh, the sun bright, and the sky so clear that it was almost possible to ignore the trash strewn about the streets, the miserable burned-out shakes, and the dilapidated houses; almost, but not quite. The city was too much of a mess.

When we arrived at the chandlery I was surprised to see Louisa talking to Philip but watching Tanka as he nailed the cover onto a large wooden box.

"Ah, Marike," she said excitedly, holding out a small cloth sack to show me. "Philip gave me some sugar. Mama will be pleased, won't she?"

I knew very well that Mrs. Bogardus would not be pleased if she thought Louisa had been to the chandlery and was about to suggest that it might be better if I carried the sugar home when I was distracted by Margretta's squeals of delight as Tanka lifted her up and sat her on the counter, where he handed her a little boat he'd carved.

"He made that out of scrap lumber," Philip said, smiling down at the child. "Can you say thank you to Tanka, Margretta?"

"Tanka, Tanka," she cried, holding the boat up for all of us to see.

"Near enough," laughed the Indian. "Now say 'boat,' little one."

Two men came into the shop just then, and the three of us left, Louisa hurrying on ahead, proudly clutching the sack of sugar.

Evidently the peace and quiet of the past few weeks was too good, or too foreign to the household, to last; the morning after our visit to the chandlery we were awakened at dawn by piercing screams interspersed with loud, hoarse cries of "Murder" coming up from the floor below us. Philip and I raced down the steep flight of stairs to Louisa's room, where Anna stood on one side of the narrow bed looking down at the slight figure of her sister, watching with horror as her mother gently and tenderly placed a pillow over the younger girl's face.

"She is dead," Anna said in a hushed voice, yanking the pillow away. "Mama—" Even though we could see that Louisa was indeed dead, Philip moved quickly to her side and checked.

"She did it, that one did it," her mother said sharply, pointing to me. "She came down in the night when we were all asleep and smothered my Louisa." Mrs. Bogardus seemed uncharacteristically calm.

"She did no such thing, and you know it, Mama," Philip interrupted. "Marike was in bed with me when . . ."

"You didn't hear her," his mother persisted. "You are a sound sleeper, Philip, always were. She slipped out—oh, she can be quiet as a mouse, that one. She did do it, she killed my beauty."

"Nonsense, Mama! Stop it at once!" Philip shouted, taking the old lady by the arm and shaking her roughly.

"The sugar, Philip, the sugar! The Indian gave her the sugar. Your wife took her to see the Indian, and then she killed her. She wanted the Indian for herself. . . ."

The arguing, the shouting, and the repeated accusations went on and on. I could still hear them when I was back up on the third floor, tending to Margretta. When Philip at last came up to get dressed he took me in his arms, kissed me all over my face, and then held me away from him. Looking down into my eyes, he spoke slowly.

"My dearest dear, I know, know absolutely, no matter what anyone says, that you never left my bed last night."

I kissed him and we stood with our arms around each other until Margretta tugged at our knees, wanting to be included.

"But who could have killed Louisa, Philip?" I asked as he picked the child up. "Who could have put a pillow over her face? Certainly not your mother or Anna. Who else is there?"

He didn't answer, and a moment later he turned away and began to dress.

"Louisa promised us, Anna and me," I went on, "that she'd never mention Tanka's name in front of your mother, but she said she *would* have to go on thinking about him. Could she have put the pillow over her own face, to be alone with her thoughts? It sounds unlikely, I know, but to get away into a world of her own where she could imagine herself with him on the cot in the back bedroom?"

"That's possible, I suppose," he said without conviction, "but no matter what happens, Marike, I am going to have Tanka take you and Margretta up to your uncle's—no, don't argue. You are in danger here."

When we went down to the kitchen Anna was standing at the sink with a cup in either hand.

"Why," she asked as soon as she saw us, "why were these two cups on Louisa's little table? She never takes—took—anything up to bed with her."

"Have you washed them, Anna?" Philip asked, reaching out for them.

"Oh, yes, I've, well, just rinsed them," she answered, looking somewhat flustered.

"Smells a little like Mama's potion, faint, though," he said after sniffing each one.

"Maybe Mama gave her something to help her sleep," Anna suggested, turning away from us, "or . . ."

"Louisa helped herself," Philip finished for her. "God only knows."

"She may have done that, Philip," I ventured. "A couple of times I did see her take a sip or two from the cup she prepared for your mother. She seemed to like the taste."

"That's it," a look of relief spreading across his face. He handed the pewter cups back to Anna. "She drank two full cups of the stuff and in her stupor suffocated herself with a pillow. She could easily have sneaked downstairs to get it after we were all asleep. She certainly knew where it was kept."

"Yes, you're right, Philip," Anna broke in quickly. "No one would have heard her. I was tired last night and went right to sleep. She would have waited until she heard Mama snoring before going down."

"But why do you suppose Mama went into her room so early?" Philip asked. "Was she in the habit of doing that, Anna?"

"Oh, yes, yes indeed. She'd wake up early herself, and thought we ought to be out of bed. Many a time she woke me up at the crack of dawn," she answered. "Louisa and I hated that. And besides, she's been checking on Louisa ever since she found her in Tanka's room."

The three of us were visibly relieved that we'd arrived at a possible, if not completely satisfactory, explanation for Louisa's death, but I still had a nagging feeling that something was missing. Later in the day when Philip was out making arrangements for his sister's burial in St. Mark's churchyard, next to her father,

I realized what it was: with the exception of the weeping and wailing of Mrs. Bogardus there'd been few tears or mourning for the death of that lovely young girl. Had there been so much killing in the war, so many deaths from starvation and disease, that we'd built up a wall of some kind against sorrow for the dead? Had death become so commonplace that we gave it no more thought than yesterday's rain? I wondered.

I didn't really want to go back to Ossining, but I knew that Philip's mind was made up and there would be no point in my arguing with him. Besides, I was sick and tired of his mother. And, I thought, maybe it wouldn't be too long before the war was over and we had our own home.

The day before Tanka was to drive us north Anna asked me to pick up a supply of the potion.

"I'd go myself, Marike," she said apologetically, "but my ankle is sore and it would hurt to walk that far."

"Can you manage, Anna, if I leave tomorrow? I could stay for—"

"No, no, you must go," she said quickly. "Philip would be angry. I'll be all right if I stay in the house. Just get Mama's potion for me. Here's some money."

I felt bad about leaving her to deal with her irascible parent and all the chores in that dark, unhappy house, and guilty that I'd be glad to be free of it all, even though it would mean being without Philip in bed beside me. Anna was right, though; Philip would be angry if I didn't go.

My earlier trips with Anna to pick up the potion had been during the winter, when I was too busy climbing over snowdrifts and trying to keep my footing to pay any attention to the outside of the widow's house. Now, in the spring, I could see that it looked attractive, almost inviting, with vines and creepers framing the doorway and trailing along the ground under the windows. There were even a few white flowers in bloom, snowdrops, I think, next to the doorstep, and to the right a neatly turned-over plot ready for planting. All so orderly, I thought, and such a contrast to the clutter and disarray of the interior of the house.

The widow greeted us pleasantly and, after giving Margretta a little sachet of dried lavender, set about preparing the potion for Mrs. Bogardus.

"And have you been keeping well?" she asked, pausing in her pounding to look up at me. "Are the rats gone?"

"Rats?" I asked blankly.

"Yes, rats," she said impatiently. "Haven't you seen them all over the city? I gave your mother-in-law a mixture of henbane and nightshade along with the potion when she came here the last time. That should take care of them. Indeed it should, for just to be sure I added a good pinch of . . ."

I couldn't hear the rest of what she said over the noise of the pounding and the squawking of a parrot, so I merely nodded. I was puzzled, though, because I knew there were no rats in the house. Of course the widow was right: they were all over the streets, and probably Mrs. Bogardus had bought the poison when she picked up her potion during that short time when she was being helpful. It struck me as strange, though, that she hadn't mentioned it to any of us. Once again, I wondered at her strange ways.

"Mama, see," Margretta called, pulling at my skirt and pointing to the brightly colored bird in a cage hanging from one of the rafters.

" 'Tis a parrot, little girl," the widow said. "A sailor gave it to me in exchange for ointments. Poor man had the scurvy; all he needed was lime or potato juice to cure it, but he would have some of my ointments."

"Do many sailors come here, ma'am?" I asked, thinking of all the ones who stopped in at the chandlery.

"Oh, yes indeed," she answered, still wielding the pounder. "They nearly always have rum to sell and many times they are willing to exchange it for potions or ointments. They don't have much money, seems like, but they keep me busy, that they do."

I bought a little packet of sweet-smelling dried flower petals to take to Tante Greta and gave no further thought to the widow's puzzling reference to henbane and nightshade until we were walking home. An animal, probably a large rat, scurried across Queen Street and disappeared under what was left of a tumbledown building, reminding me of what the widow Riddell had said. I didn't know whether to mention the window's comment to Anna, and by the time we reached the Bogardus house I still hadn't made up my mind.

I might have said something that night at supper, but Philip talked so much and so excitedly about how money was being made by investing in cargo ships that I forgot about rats and poisons. As I watched his mother's eyes shine at the thought of being wealthy, I had to wonder what she would spend the money on: servants, jewels? Oh, I didn't know. How could I possibly have known what went on in that crazy mind of hers? And what could she have done with the rat poison? I had developed a disturbing theory of my own, but I said nothing to anyone.

When Tanka, Margretta, and I left early the next day for Ossining I still had not told a soul about the widow's remarks. Should I have? The fact that I did not still worries me. How many times have I asked myself if keeping silent about the truth is the same as telling a lie?

Chapter Ten

I did not hear of the death of my parents until after our son, Adrien, was born. Philip brought me the news on an unusually warm day in late October 1781, when the fields and gardens surrounding the farmhouse glowed in the lovely autumnal light.

" 'Twas the fever, Marike," he said quietly, putting his arms around me as we stood looking down at the infant in his cradle. "Typhoid, probably."

"But my mother always boiled the water she got from the well, Philip."

"Or it could have been the cholera," he continued. "They've both been terrible these past months. The preachers say it's punishment for our evil ways, but I say that's nonsense. It's the filth in the city; the rats and vermin cause all the sickness. And, of course, one person passes it on to the next one."

"Did they suffer, Philip? Do you know?"

"No, I don't, my love, but the neighbor I spoke to, the one

who found them, said they both looked peaceful, lying side by side in the bed."

"And they've been buried?"

"Yes, and they still lie side by side. Tanka helped me dig the graves. The pastor who read the service said the one man he had left had been taken sick and he didn't know when he'd find another. No one wanted the job, he told me. They are all afraid of the sickness."

"Oh, Philip, I am so grateful to you and Tanka. I couldn't bear to think of them lying neglected. . . ."

"Don't cry, love. They're probably happier now in some bright place—maybe a heavenly pear orchard—than they ever were on earth."

The thought of my hardworking father and mother wandering hand in hand through Wiltwyck's orchard made me smile, and that made Philip kiss me and hold me close to him until Tante Greta called us to come down to supper.

"Now I feel like a real grossmoeder," she said, looking around the kitchen table. "Just imagine, I have not one but two klein-kinder! It makes me so happy!"

I have seldom seen a woman as cheerful as my aunt was that night, not even during the two years I spent with her and Uncle Franz; nor have I seen as sorrowful a one as she was when Philip took me back to New York in the fall of 1783, the year the British evacuated our city. Even promises to return the following summer did nothing to cheer her, nor did they keep away the tears that were never far from the surface during our last few days in Ossining. When we were leaving she suddenly looked so old, so sad and miserable, that if the wagon had not already started to roll down the narrow lane I might have jumped out and, and done what? I don't know.

Although Cornwallis had been defeated in Yorktown on the nineteenth of October, 1781, New York remained under British domination until 1783, when General Washington returned triumphantly. During that two-year interval, Loyalists, some say as many as sixty thousand of them, fled the city. While some sailed back to England and others headed for Nova Scotia and Canada proper, patriots who had left New York in 1775 streamed back into Manhattan to reclaim their property and were almost overcome by anger and despair at the sight of the desecration that greeted them on their return. Houses had been ransacked, and anything that could be used for firewood had been reduced to ashes. Tables, chairs, beds, even the wooden shutters we used to close so carefully at night, all—all were gone.

"They burned everything they could get their hands on in order to keep warm and cook their food," Philip said, trying to prepare me for the sight that awaited us. "I wanted to have your parents' house ready for us to move into, but it's still an empty shell. There's nothing in it but the kitchen range. The British must have had enough stoves, I guess. So we'll have to live on Water Street for a while. I know you weren't happy there, love, but it won't be long. I could have waited to bring you back, but I wanted you here before the snow starts. It's safe enough in the Water Street house; we've been free of robbers and scavengers because of Anna's Britisher. You know, the man who was courting her. Somehow his presence kept the marauding soldiers away. And I promise you, my darling, as soon as the house on Beaver Street is habitable we'll move into it."

"Did Anna marry her soldier?" I asked.

"No, and maybe it's just as well she didn't, because he took off for England shortly after the defeat at Yorktown. He realized how antagonistic the patriots were to all British citizens and didn't want to put up with it. Anna is despondent, unhappy, sometimes furious at everything and everyone. She reminds me of my mother—oh, poor girl! I feel sorry for her; she loved him and trusted him and believed all the promises he made. Empty promises . . ."

"Why didn't I ever see him when I was living there with Margretta, Philip?"

"He was away with his regiment then, love, with Howe's army. I met him several times, but that must have been before you came and after Tanka took you back to Ossining. He seemed to be all right, but I thought he was one of those fellows always out for themselves. He was a lieutenant, and Anna, of course, was madly in love with him. She was completely crushed when he left without saying anything about taking her with him or coming back to her."

"What was his name?"

"Hugh Saunders. A big fellow, good-looking, liked to tell stories about his life in England. In the early days he would flirt with Louisa—you remember how pretty she was—but it was Anna he courted."

She would have made a good wife, I thought, as we rattled along, remembering how she bustled about, managing that strange household, seeing to the meals, the laundry, the cleaning, and the needs of her mother. How can she stand it? And, I wondered, how will I be able to stand it a second time?

As if he knew what was going on in my mind, Philip leaned over to give me a quick kiss.

"I'll say it again, love: I promise you we'll move into your old home as soon as possible, maybe within a month. It will have to be thoroughly cleaned, and we'll need to find furnishings, beds, chairs and the rest. I have some paint for the walls, and Tanka is ready to help. It won't be long."

Chapter Eleven

I do not know what Philip meant by "long," and perhaps he wasn't sure himself, but "interminable" would have been a better word for the months that followed. I wish I could say there were some happy times during that period. Maybe there were and I've forgotten them because they were overshadowed by the dark, dull winter days and the almost palpable unhappiness of Anna and the gloomy presence of Mrs. Bogardus.

"She never got over Louisa's death," Philip said when I told him that his mother spent her days sitting in front of the small fire in the grate muttering to herself. "And Anna's no help. Ever since Saunders left she's gone around like a lost soul; you must have noticed how she won't even speak if she can help it. I tried to persuade her to go out, meet some people, but she won't. I even brought a fellow home, a good man, thinking she might like him, but she closed herself in her room. Maybe it's just as well she did; that sour expression on her face would have scared him off anyway."

Anna had never been a beauty, but in earlier days she'd had

a rather attractive appearance. Now the once bright, laughing eyes were dull, the lips that had smiled so readily were set in a firm, straight line, and the light blond hair that had gleamed in sun and firelight looked drab and neglected. She must have stopped brushing it.

"Anna doesn't look well," I said when Philip paused, "but when I asked her if she had a headache or a pain she just shook her head and turned away."

"Leave her to herself, Marike. They say no one ever died of love. She'll come out of it in time, and we'll be out of here by the spring. Then she and my mother can work things out for themselves."

"Your mother won't like that, Philip. She's always been afraid you'd leave her. She doesn't care a bit about me or the children, or about Anna, for that matter."

"Well, you and my son and daughter are the ones I care about, and Water Street is not the place for any of you. Enough talking, love. Come to bed now, it's late."

Anna continued to retire more and more into herself and Mrs. Bogardus went on with her solitary brooding. She rarely spoke and seldom moved from her chair in the front room; that is until the night before Philip and I left her house for good, at which time all her stored-up resentment of me burst forth in a manner that left us all shaken. The four of us were sitting quietly (I don't know about Anna and Philip, but I couldn't think of anything appropriate to say) while Tanka waited in the kitchen for Philip's instructions concerning the opening of the shop the next day. Suddenly Mrs. Bogardus broke the silence.

"Now I will speak out," she began in a voice that was somewhat hoarse and at the same time severe and threatening, "and you will hear me out. This is what I have to say: since my only son is deserting me to live with a thief and a murderess, I must take action. . . ."

"Enough, Mama!" Philip commanded. "Stop right now!"

"No! I will not stop!" she cried. "You cannot make me stop. She stole my silver ring, she killed my beautiful Louisa, she brought an Indian into my house! She is worse than bad: she is evil and she must be punished. Evil deserves punishment!"

By this time she was on her feet, ready to spring at me, I thought, but instead of coming toward me, she suddenly bent over and picked up the pewter pitcher that always stood on the table next to her chair. Seconds later, as she raised her arm to hurl the heavy object at me, Tanka, who had come silently into the room while she was shouting, leaned over and grasped her forearm so firmly that the pitcher fell from her hand and landed on the floor. When she turned to see who had prevented her taking the revenge she sought, Tanka was nowhere to be seen.

"My God! She could have killed you!" Philip gasped, clasping me to him. "Are you all right, love?"

I couldn't answer; all I could do was nod as silence descended on the room while Anna, Philip, and I stood watching the old lady stare blankly at the hand that had held the pewter pitcher.

As we left, I couldn't help thinking that although the old lady's outbursts seemed to have diminished in frequency, this last one had been truly horrifying. It was only because I was finally leaving Water Street to go to my own home that I was able to put it out of my mind.

Chapter Twelve

B y 1784 the city was making a concerted effort to recover from the dreadful condition to which the British occupation had brought it. Churches and warehouses the Loyalists had used as prisons were either refurbished or demolished, old houses were torn down and rebuilt, and new ones sprang up to the north of us. Efforts were made (not always successful) to clean the streets, and wherever possible the names the British had given them were changed. Instead of King Street we now had Pine Street. Queen Street became Pearl, Crown Street was changed to Liberty, and when Kings College was reorganized it became Columbia. I have to admit that though the delight we took in wiping out all traces of the Loyalists may seem childish now, it was mighty satisfying then. Returning citizens reclaimed their property, merchants opened up their shops again, and trade began to prosper. So did we.

I have mentioned that for some time Philip had been buying shares in various merchant ships, a few here, a few there, and by the time the *Empress of China*, the ship that opened the Orient to American traders, returned from her maiden voyage in May of 1785, we were fairly well off. The *Empress*, as she was called, had sailed from New York carrying large quantities of furs, woolens, and ginseng, a root highly prized by the Chinese, since it was said to strengthen male virility. She returned with a cargo of tea, silks, nankeen, and china. I still have and cherish a set of fragile cups and plates from that first voyage.

As I said, by that time we were fairly well off, although it had taken months of hard work to transform the Beaver Street house into a comfortable, orderly dwelling place, but by the time Philip brought home the set of china for me I was satisfied with my surroundings. However, I was no longer satisfied with the state of my marriage, and now that I've had plenty of time to think things over I can see that I acted stupidly.

When our third child, a tiny girl, was stillborn after a long and difficult labor, I told Philip that I did not wish to be brought to childbed again. I realized later that I never should have withheld sex from him; it wasn't fair to him, although he said he understood and didn't complain at all. I was the unhappy one.

"I hope I'm not wearing out my welcome, Marike," Anna said when she appeared at my door one warm July afternoon, "but it's so good to get away from Mama for a few hours. You're the only one I can talk to about how difficult she makes my life. It seems as if the feebler she becomes, the more demanding she is. I know it's wrong, but sometimes I wish she'd die."

At first I didn't mind listening to her as we sat in the small garden behind the house while I kept an eye on Margretta and Adrien and caught up on the mending, but when Anna's visits became more and more frequent I grew tired of hearing the same things over and over again.

"Anna's becoming more and more like your mother," I said to Philip one evening after the children were in bed. "She does nothing but complain from the moment she steps through the door."

"Poor thing," he said gravely. "I feel sorry for her, but what can I do? What can anyone do?"

"Oh, I feel sorry for her, too, Philip, and I try to think of things to say to cheer her up, but she just turns away or says that I don't know what I'm talking about. What will she do when your mother dies? How old is your mother now?"

"Fifty or fifty-one, I think."

"Well, when she does go, Anna will be free of her, but that will mean she'll be completely alone."

"I think we'll have to take her in, Marike. I think she expects that. I am her brother, you know."

Oh, no, I thought, keeping my eyes on my knitting.

"That won't happen for a while, though," Philip continued, putting aside the toy he was mending for Adrien, "and when we move into a larger house things shouldn't be too bad. Did I tell you I have my eye on some lots up on Elizabeth Street? You must come and see them and tell me what you think.

"In the meantime, I suppose it wouldn't hurt if I stopped in at Water Street for a half hour or so after I close the shop. Maybe that would take a little of the strain off Anna."

"Your mother would like it," I said. "Yes, I think—"

"Wait, Marike, listen," he interrupted. "I know Anna's visits are tiresome for you. Why don't you and the children go up to Ossining? Get out of the heat and away from Anna? There's a stage to Albany now; you wouldn't have to travel in a wagon."

"Yes, I would like that," I said after a moment or two. "I've heard several people say they're leaving the city for the summer for fear of sickness. They say the yellow fever can spread so quickly in hot weather. Will you come with us?"

"That's just it, love. The shop is busy, and I want to spend as much time as I can at the counting house. Tanka and Adam can manage for short periods of time, an hour or so, but I wouldn't like to leave them for several days. The money is coming in now, Marike, and I want to keep it coming."

A change came over him when he began to speak of money; his voice sharpened, his eyes lit up as if he could see gold pieces pouring into his coffers, and for a moment I was reminded of his mother's expression the night he'd spoken of being wealthy. I remember thinking, He always has money on his mind these days, and now he wants me to go away. . . .

I did go to Ossining with the children for the rest of that summer, and a week after my return in September, Anna resumed her visits to Beaver Street. She had the same stream of complaints about life with her mother, but that fall I hardly listened to her because my mind was on my renewed happiness with Philip. Tante Greta was responsible for that. She knew something was bothering me, and when I told her about the state of my marriage she shook her head and said it was not right that I should deny Philip my body.

"He needs you, Marike," she declared, "and you must comply with his wishes or else he might stray. You would not like that, would you? And who can tell, all pregnancies are not hard. Besides, you are older now; you might not conceive."

I still remember Philip's delight when I told him I no longer feared another birth. He immediately became tender and loving again, the Philip with whom I had lain on the riverbank years ago, the man with whom I was still in love.

"You just needed a respite, my darling," he said, pulling me to him and gently caressing my breasts. Then he chuckled before continuing: "I think I will send you to Ossining any time I feel you are drawing away from me."

I knew I'd been unhappy, but I didn't realize until that moment how much I had missed our lovemaking.

"Marike, you are not paying attention to me," Anna cried one gray afternoon when we were sitting by the fire in the front room. "You are smiling a little secret smile while I am telling you how hard it is for me."

I had actually been paying no attention at all to Anna's repeated accounts of her mother's behavior, but when she began to harp on how lucky I was to have my own home and family I could not help but listen.

"And you have your aunt and uncle," she was saying resentfully. "I have no relations, no country place to go to in the heat of the summer. You've told me how wondereful Ossining is, but Marike, if I were you I wouldn't leave my husband alone in the city for weeks on end. Philip is just like other men; he knows where to go to satisfy his desires."

"Anna!" I exclaimed. "What are you talking about? Philip?"

"You know perfectly well what I am talking about. Don't pretend you are not aware of the houses of pleasure, some of them quite close by," she said with a knowing look.

"No, I don't know what you're talking about," I said sharply, standing up and starting for the kitchen.

"You'll see," she called after me. "You'll find out."

I made no reply, and a few minutes later I heard the front door slam.

I often told Philip about Anna's visits and her complaints, but I never repeated that conversation to him or to anyone else.

Anna did not come back to see me for three whole weeks, for which I was grateful. When she finally did return, she once again accused me of not listening to her.

"I'm sorry, Anna," I said apologetically, "I was thinking of something."

"Yes, you were thinking of something happy. You have everything to be happy about, my brother, the little ones—what do I have?"

Before I could respond she burst into tears, and then, still sobbing, burst out:

"I hate her! If I could kill her and not be found out I would do it in a minute!"

I waited until she calmed down a little and then suggested that perhaps we could find someone to stay with Mrs. Bogardus so that Anna could have some time for herself.

"Someone to do the housework," I said, "and sit with her."

"Oh, she wouldn't stand for that!" Anna exclaimed. "How many times have I heard her say: 'No strangers in my house'? She wants *me* there, at her beck and call. I have to sneak out to come here when she takes her nap. Yes, I'm the one she wants, and she's only content when she's making me miserable."

She began to cry again, this time more softly, and when I reached over to pat her on the back, she clutched my hand.

"It isn't only that, Marike," she said tearfully, "not just Mama. It's the loneliness. Oh, I am so alone! I have no one, no one. If only there were someone, anyone."

Before I could think of any comforting words she stood up, wiped her eyes, and left without another word.

When Philip came in that evening he looked so tired that I hesitated to tell him about Anna's visit. It would only upset him to hear that she thought of killing her mother, and he had enough on his mind as it was. She didn't really mean that, I said to myself. At least I hoped she didn't.

I didn't see Anna again for almost three months, and although at times I felt a bit guilty about enjoying my afternoons without her, I didn't know what I could do to help her. Philip refused to let me go over to Water Street—of course he was right—and after a while I tried not to think about her. I had other things on my mind, anyway: taking care of the house and the children, feeding the four of us (sometimes five, for Tanka was a frequent visitor), seeing to the laundry, and doing the shopping. The shops had so much better fare to offer than they'd had during the war, and so I was able to introduce some variety into our meals. This delighted Margretta and Adrien, and even Philip, who seldom paid much attention to food, noticed an improvement in our diet.

"Where did you buy such tasty meat, Marike?" he asked one night at supper when I served particularly juicy, tender slices of pot roast.

"Down on Dock Street there's a butcher shop," I answered. "A German named Heinrich Astor owns it. My friend Eliza Warren—you remember meeting her—she's the one who went to the

Dames' School years ago. She told me he had good meat, so I went there with her this morning. He introduced us to his brother Jacob, a strange man if I ever saw one. Of course he's a German, too, but he's just recently come here from England. He, Jacob, I mean, showed us some flutes he had for sale and then brought out a pile of furs, beaver, I think, that he offered us."

"Must be the same man," Philip said, putting down his knife and fork and sitting back in his chair. "He came into the chandlery late today, carrying some furs—must have sold the flutes—wanting information about ships sailing for England. Said he had a large supply of beaver and muskrat skins to send. He seemed like a fellow out to make a pile of money."

Philip certainly sized up Jacob Astor correctly: it wasn't long before Mr. Astor was one of the richest men—if not *the* richest man—in New York.

"Did you see Anna when you stopped in at your mother's today?" I asked later that evening.

"No, she stayed in the kitchen. My mother was drinking her potion and didn't have much to say, so I didn't stay long. Sometimes I wonder why I bother to go at all; I'd much rather come right home. Look, love, do you feel like a little reading tonight? Did Eliza lend you another book?"

I nodded and handed him volume 1 of Mr. Swift's *Gulliver's Travels*. I smiled to myself, remembering how when I first visited Eliza Warren's house I could not get over the number of books arranged on shelves in a small room in the rear of her house. She explained that her father had made a point of collecting them, buying them, one at a time, whenever he could.

"This house was his home," she'd said, "and when he died three years ago it came to me. James and I have left things pretty much as they were, especially the books. I've been reading some of them. Marike, you might like to, too. Try this one, it's a good story. Here, take it with you, but be sure to bring it back."

It *was* a good story, and for the next several weeks Philip and I took turns reading aloud in the evenings Mr. Defoe's account of the adventures of Robinson Crusoe and his man Friday. Since I knew how precious the book was to Eliza I made a little cloth cover for it to make sure that no harm came to the dark red leather binding, a cover that, strangely enough, fitted most of the volumes on her shelves. It was used constantly over the next two or three years as we made our way through the novels of Richardson, Fielding, Smollett, and Sterne. Philip liked most of these, particularly *The History of Tom Jones*, but he had no use for *Tristram Shandy*. When he found a copy of Mr. Walpole's *Castle of Otranto* in a bookseller's on Pine Street he brought it home, saying it would serve as the beginning of our own library. I still have our copy of *Otranto* and reread parts of it when I feel the need of entertainment.

When I finished a chapter the other day I sat with the book on my lap thinking of the huge debt I owe Eliza Warren for introducing me to the world of literature. The only book I ever saw in my parents' house when I was growing up was my father's ledger.

Chapter Thirteen

W e have news for you, Marike," Philip called out as he and Tanka came in for supper one evening late in February 1786. "Hugh Saunders is back. Remember the fellow who was courting Anna? He landed today and Anna's walking on air. I've never seen such a change in anyone."

"Britisher, big man," added Tanka, who was making a great show of shaking hands solemnly with Margretta and Adrien.

"Is he here to stay, Philip?"

"Possibly. He's no longer in the British army, so I guess he can live wherever he likes. I wasn't talking to him for more than a few minutes, but I got the impression that things didn't work out too well for him in England, so he left."

"Well, I'm glad for Anna's sake, but what about your mother? How does she feel about having a stranger in the house?"

"Oh, she made it clear that he couldn't stay there, and he very quickly assured her that he had no such intention. In spite of the way he treated my sister a while back, he's very well mannered, Marike, and managed to quiet Mama down better than I ever could. He even flattered her a bit, commenting on the beauty of the pin she was wearing, that old amethyst one, saying how the color became her and so on. I think that when he stood up and put a cushion under her arm—it was trembling—he was making a definite effort to win her over. She even smiled at him."

"Perhaps he'll stay in one of the boarding houses. Mrs. Todd is said to run a good one."

"Yes, but who can tell what my mother will do? He might persuade her to rent him a room. He was lodged there for a time during the war, you know, so he's not quite a stranger."

Although Philip did not say he mistrusted Hugh Saunders, I could tell he was not completely easy in his mind concerning the Britisher. Then, when I suddenly remembered Anna's tearful wish for someone, anyone, I hoped Saunders would make her happy. When she brought him to see us one blustery evening in March, though, I was not so sure that he would.

"My, you have a beautiful wife and a cozy home for yourself, Philip," Hugh Saunders said shortly after the four of us were seated in the front room. "A good fire going, one that warms us all, not just those up close to it."

"Oh, Hugh," Anna protested. "You know Mama can't help worrying about running out of coal."

"Of course she can't, my love, but it certainly feels good to be warm after our windy walk over here. And I must say, Marike, this mulled cider really adds to our comfort."

Anna looked hurt for a moment or two, as if she were being

blamed for her mother's shortcomings, but when Hugh leaned over and took her hand in his she perked up again.

"Philip," Saunders was saying when I turned my attention back to him, "do you know of any quick way to make a few pounds, or preferably guineas?"

"Guineas are somewhat rare these days, Hugh," Philip said dryly, "and the only way I know to make any money is to work for it."

"Not really accustomed to hard labor, friend," drawled Saunders, "but my severance pay won't last forever. Thought you might hear of something over in that shop of yours."

"I'll let you know if I do," Philip said shortly before turning to talk to Anna, who had been looking rather anxiously from one man to the other.

I tried to draw Hugh out about his life in England after his return in 1781 but he was not forthcoming. All I learned was that he thought King George was a lunatic and that the trouble with France was making life difficult for everyone.

"I can't do anything for that fellow," Philip said crossly one evening about a month after the visit from Anna and Saunders. "I suggested that he get in touch with Astor because I heard he was hiring people, but Saunders said no thanks, he had no desire to trek through the woods looking for animal skins. Then he proposed that I take him on as a partner in the chandlery. You should have seen Tanka's face when he heard that."

"He could probably find work with one of the builders," I said.

"Oh, no, not Saunders. No indeed, he might get his hands dirty."

"But how can he manage? What is he living on, Philip?"

"Not what, but who? He's living on Anna and my mother, that's who.

"He's living on my mother's money. She pays for everything with the money I give her. You see, my father left the chandlery to me with the stipulation that I give my mother one half the profits each month for as long as she lives, and I've been doing that, paying her on the first day of each month. He said nothing about Anna or Louisa; I guess he assumed they'd marry and be taken care of that way. The money I make investing in cargo ships is completely separate; it is mine—ours—to keep, and I will see that Saunders never gets his hands on it.

"He's no good, Marike. He's living in the Water Street house, supposedly renting a room, but is he paying for it? I ask you! And Anna waits on him hand and foot. Oh, he knows a good berth when he sees one."

"Have they spoken of marriage?"

"Yes, a little, but he says they have to wait until he's—what's that word?—oh, yes, 'established.' That's what he said. As I see it he's 'established' himself in Water Street and intends to stay there."

Chapter Fourteen

As time went on we more or less accepted the situation over on Water Street, although Philip said "accepted" was not the right word for the attitude we took.

"I think 'accustomed' is a better word, Marike. Yes, that's it. We've become accustomed to Saunders's presence there. Hmm, I wonder," he mused as he sipped his cider after supper one night.

I think he had become interested in using the exact or correct word in a sentence as a result of all the reading we'd been doing. At that particular time we were well into *Joseph Andrews*, but before we could finish Mr. Fielding's delightful novel several events took place that caused us to put it aside.

I was out doing my errands one cold morning in February 1788 when I decided to stop in at the chandlery to warm my hands and feet for a few minutes before going on, and that was when I first became aware of the trouble Hugh Saunders was causing. Anna was talking to Philip in a low, excited voice in back of the shop while Tanka filled an order for the supply officer of one of the ships in the harbor.

"What can I do?" I heard her say as I stepped behind the counter. "He won't let me . . . Oh, Marike! I don't know, I just don't know. . . ."

"Marike," Philip broke in, "see if you can make any sense of this. Come, we can talk in here." He opened the door to the storeroom, in one corner of which Tanka's cot was partially hidden by curtains made of sailcloth, and pulled out two stools for us.

"Now, Anna, tell me," I said as gently as I could.

"There's a man, I don't know who he is," she began nervously. "He stands out in front, looking at the house. I came out the back way, so he wouldn't see me. When Hugh saw him from the window he was so angry. He swore terribly. I can't . . ."

She burst into tears and, ignoring the stool, sank down on a packing case, unable to go on. After a moment or two Philip leaned over, patted her shoulder, and said softly: "Do you think Hugh recognized the man, Anna?"

"I think he must have," she said haltingly. "He pulled me away from the window—he hurt my arm—and when Mama asked who it was he told her to be still. Then Mama cried, and he yelled at her. He'd always been so nice to her. And then when I asked him if the man was dangerous, he swore again and hit me! Oh, what will I do? I thought he loved me and would marry me. I was waiting and waiting."

"Stop crying, Anna," Philip said brusquely, "and come with me. I'll see who this fellow is. Marike, you go home; I'll be there later."

It was dark and I had already given Margretta and Adrien their supper when Philip arrived home accompanied by Tanka and a tall, middle-aged man.

"This is Mr. Robert Cutler of Lancashire, England, Marike. My wife, sir."

"My apologies for intruding on you at this hour, madam," Mr. Cutler said in a gruff but not unpleasant voice, "but your husband has been good enough to undertake to help me solve a problem that has weighed heavily on my mind for some months now, and we have plans to make."

"What happened, Philip? Is everything all right?" I asked.

"Yes, yes, and Saunders is gone," he answered. "We'll tell you, but first some food. Is there enough?"

Fortunately, I had cooked a large pot of beef and vegetables, and that, with plenty of bread and butter and apple pudding, satisfied their appetites.

"What it amounts to, Marike," Philip said once we were seated in the front room, "is this: Mr. Cutler is looking for Hugh Saunders, who married his daughter and then deserted her."

"It was an elopement, ma'am," the Englishman said, taking up the tale. "Charlotte, my daughter, my only child, was but seventeen years of age when Saunders came to work for me. He had references (which later turned out to be forgeries) and seemed capable. I needed an overseer at that time, someone who could manage men and who knew horses, and from the start I was pleased with the way Saunders performed.

"I had no idea he was seeing Charlotte other than in my company, except, of course, when they went riding together. He was teaching her, he said, some of the finer points of horsemanship. That was not all he taught her. The day came when I found her crying hysterically in the arms of my housekeeper, and when she could speak she told me they'd been married by a preacher in the next county, that she was with child, and that Saunders was gone."

"When was this?" Philip asked.

"Almost a year ago, sir," answered Mr. Cutler. "Charlotte miscarried at four months, which is probably just as well, but she has never been the same. Oh, physically she's fine and healthy, but she cries and mopes around the place, longing for that rascal, until I'm nearly crazy.

"One of the stable hands used to go drinking with Saunders and heard him say several times that New York was the place where fortunes were made, and when Charlotte heard that, nothing would satisfy her but that I come here to find him! And there are other reasons why I made the trip: not only do I see red every time I think of how he took advantage of my daughter, but also when I remember that he was a despicable, lying thief. He stole over a hundred pounds I had on hand, and not only that, he forged my name on bank drafts for two thousand pounds! I had been contemplating the purchase of some land adjoining my acres. Yes, two thousand pounds! Now, I am a fairly wealthy man, but still . . .

"He also stole the priceless portrait Sir Joshua painted of my dear wife before she took sick. Oh, yes, I have my own score to settle with Hugh Saunders."

"How did you know to look for him on Water Street, Mr. Cutler?" I asked.

"Pure chance, madam. Sometimes of an evening Saunders would speak of his wartime experiences, and once or twice he mentioned being billeted with a family named Geradus, at least

I thought that was the name. So when I came here, a month ago now, I searched and eventually found a family of that name, but they'd never heard of him. They said they knew of no other Geradus but that there was a Bogardus on Water Street. There was indeed, but I could not gain entrance. I'm pretty sure, actually *very* sure, that I saw Saunders in the window."

"I'm sure you did, too, Mr. Cutler," Philip said, "but by the time Anna and I got there he'd disappeared. Went out the back way and took off. He could be hiding anywhere or even gone to sea. Two ships, the *Maria D.* and the *Sea Bird*, sailed this evening."

"Or he may be back in Water Street," I said. "He knows Anna will hide him."

"Your sister-in-law would be a fool to do that," the Englishman said dryly.

"People in love have been known to do foolish things," I reminded him.

The embarrassing silence that followed my remark was broken by Tanka's eager voice:

"Philip, I look for this Saunders. You want me to look?"

"Yes, certainly, Tanka. It would help if you did," Philip responded. "I'll talk to you about it later. In the meantime we'll try to think of what else to do."

I excused myself at that point to see to the children and did not go downstairs again that night. After a while I heard footsteps in the attic above our room, and when Philip came up to bed he explained that from now on Tanka was to sleep in our house.

"Why on earth?"

"As a safeguard, love. No one knows what Saunders might

do or where he'll go. I didn't like the way he kept looking at you when he was here that night or the way he seemed to be examining the place, as if he thought of moving in."

"Your mother's house offers much better hiding places."

"True, true, but don't forget this: he had his way with Charlotte Cutler and maybe, I don't know for sure but I suspect it, with Anna. And you, my love, are a far more desirable woman than my sister."

"What will Tanka sleep on? There's no bed up in the attic."

"I found some quilts in an old trunk; the British must have missed them when they ransacked the place. Tomorrow Tanka can bring his cot and whatever else he has over from the chandlery. Don't worry about him, love; Tanka could sleep on an ice floe if he had to."

The constables who patrolled the streets during the daytime (there weren't very many of them) and the members of the night watch were given descriptions of Hugh Saunders and told to arrest him for theft. He had not only robbed Mr. Cutler before he left England, but Anna discovered that several articles were missing from the Water Street house: a gold chain belonging to her mother, a set of six silver teaspoons that were kept wrapped in flannel and never used, and a locket her father had given her years ago.

"There may be other things missing," she said when she stopped in one afternoon while Mrs. Bogardus took her nap, "things I haven't thought to look for. Oh, Marike! How could he do it? He said he loved me, and I loved him . . . I still love him! And he made Mama happy; he used to tell her she was wonderful. Oh, how could he say that? She's awful. She believed it, though, and the more he flattered her the more she smiled. She never smiles at me. I even saw her patting his hand. Can you believe that?"

"Did she give him money, Anna?"

"I don't know. Maybe, but I never saw her do it." She frowned, thought for a moment, and then said: "She may have, because sometimes he'd go out to play cards and come home with money he said he'd won. He'd have needed some money to start with, wouldn't he?"

I nodded but didn't say anything. I wanted to tell her to forget about him, but I doubt that she would have heard me if I did.

"Oh, Marike," she wailed, "I miss him so much! I know he's a rascal, but I want him to come back. He could be so loving, and he did keep Mama from driving me crazy. I could have murdered her this morning when she scratched my arm because I gave her the blue shawl instead of the black one. Look, you can see where it was bleeding."

"Let me bind it up for you, Anna."

"No, no, it's all right now, but it did hurt, and for a moment I thought I might be going mad. I caught myself thinking how easy it would be to kill her. Maybe I am going mad?"

"You mustn't say such things, Anna. You are not going mad. You were upset and exasperated, and I don't blame you. Your mother is an extremely difficult person."

"If Hugh came back—but why do I want him now? They say he's married to a girl in England. Why did he say we'd be married? Do you think he'll come back?"

Anna continued on in this vein, hardly pausing long enough for me to reply, which was just as well, since I was at a loss for words. When the clock struck four she jumped up and hurried out, leaving me to wonder whether both mother and daughter weren't slightly mad. And then, of course, there was still the question of Louisa.

Chapter Fifteen

I do not like to think about the dreadful, horrible hours I lived through during the days following Anna's last visit to Beaver Street, and I have therefore time after time put off writing about them. Now, however, I know that this record would be incomplete without an account of some kind, and I will try to give an accurate one.

To the delight of Margretta and Adrien, Tanka arrived every evening and set out for work with Philip the following morning after breakfast. He took his responsibility as our guardian seriously; when Philip had business that kept him at the chandlery after dark, Tanka made sure the two doors and all the windows and shutters were firmly locked before sitting down to wait for the sound of my husband's footsteps on the stone stoop. Had the Indian with his keen ears and sharp eyes been there in the daytime, things might have been different.

At first I didn't recognize the tall, bearded man wearing a black knitted cap well down over his forehead who fell into step beside me when I was carrying my pails of water home from the well at the corner. I must have looked startled because before I could say a word he spoke sharply.

"Don't cry out and no harm will come to you. Give me one of the pails to carry, as if I were an old friend. We will go to the rear door of your house; that's where you take the water in, isn't it?"

I nodded my head, trying to swallow the sudden fear that was building up inside me, and walked as steadily as I could down our narrow street and along the path that led to the back door.

"Open it!" he commanded. "Get inside quickly. Put the pail down and get me some food. Hurry!"

I thought I'd heard the voice before, but it wasn't until he'd pulled his cap off and tossed it on the table that I recognized Hugh Saunders. He didn't look at all like the nicely dressed Englishman who had come to call with Anna that one time, not at all like him. On that occasion he'd been clean-shaven and healthy-looking; this time he was shabbily dressed in a coat that was torn at one sleeve and stained down the front. His eyes were bloodshot and his hair unkempt. Besides, he smelled as if he hadn't washed recently.

"What are you staring at?" he asked harshly. "Get on with it. Put some food in front of me."

Maybe he'll go away if I feed him, I thought wildly as I took out bread and cheese with hands that had begun to shake. After pouring him a mug of cider, I stood still and waited until he'd eaten all the cheese and half the loaf I'd baked the day before to ask him if he would please leave.

"That will depend," he said, looking at me intently. "Have you an attic here?"

"Yes, that's where Tanka sleeps."

"Ah, yes, the Indian. Well then, we must go."

"We? What—"

"Yes, we. You will come with me and stay with me, unless you die, of course, until your husband and Cutler agree to my conditions, which are all spelled out here."

He took a piece of folded paper from a pocket in his coat and laid it on the table, anchoring it with my sugar bowl.

"No! Don't touch that!" he hissed, grabbing my arm painfully as I reached out to pick up the paper.

"Let go!" I cried. "You're hurting me!"

"You'll be hurt more than that if you don't do as I say. Come, now, it's time we were away."

"I can't go anyplace; I must be here when the children come home from school."

Then I remembered that Philip had said they could both go to the chandlery to help Adam polish the brasses, but I kept that information to myself.

"You're coming with me," Saunders said sharply.

"I'll leave a note," I began, thinking I could alert Philip.

"Oh no you won't," he said, pulling me away from the table. "And don't try to get away from me. I have strong hands and a stronger temper. Now, get that knitted blanket or whatever it is I saw on the back of a chair in the other room. You'll need it at the Points."

I hurried out of the kitchen, thinking I could make a dash for the front door, but he was right behind me, almost on top of me, and any attempt to escape would have been futile. There was nothing for me to do but to roll up the afghan and hug it close to my chest as we made our way through the house and out the back door into the cold air.

"Stop," I said suddenly. "The buckle on my shoe is undone. I must fix it."

He let go of my arm but stood over me as I bent down, pretending to adjust the buckle. He'd said "the Points," I remembered, and that could only mean the Five Points, a deadful place. I picked up a small stone and with the hand that was partly covered by the afghan quickly scratched the number *five* on the piece of slate in front of the door. A poor substitute for a note, but maybe . . .

I knew that the Five Points was located where Cross, Anthony, Orange, Little Water, and Mulberry Streets came together, and that the small park in the middle of it was called Paradise Square. That was where poor people used to go on Sundays and holidays for recreation. I also knew that Collect Pond was nearby, and that the widow Riddell lived not far from that. If, I thought, I could get away from Saunders, maybe I could—but at that moment he jerked my arm and told me to hurry along, and I forgot all about the widow.

What I did not know about the Five Points was that shoddy-looking dwellings (you could hardly call them houses) had sprung up after the war was over and had already begun to deteriorate.

It was to one of these that Saunders led me, a three-story building that seemed to lean against the one next to it. Some of the
broken windows had been covered over with boards, and the door
of the one we were approaching swung crazily back and forth in
the wind.

"Is this where we're going?" I asked, horrified by what I saw.

He must have sensed my disgust because he picked me up
and carried me into a hallway where the smell of excrement was
almost overpowering. "Now walk," he ordered, setting me down
on the lowest step of a flight of dark, unswept stairs. "Go on, all
the way up to the top floor."

The stairway was narrow and some of the treads were broken, causing me to stumble as I climbed. I wanted to turn
around, push Saunders out of the way, and run as fast as I could,
but he was close behind me, shoving me along. As we rose higher
in that awful building I heard coarse voices, shouts, and loud
coughing mixed with drunken laughter, and when we reached
the second floor a screaming woman, followed by shouts and
curses, lurched past us and disappeared into the darkness somewhere to my left. That frightened me more than anything Saunders had said or done so far, and I began to cry. I was too tired
and miserable to even try to wrench my arm away from his cruel
grasp, to try to think of a means of escape, and close to giving in
to a deep, deep despair.

The room into which he guided me on the third floor was
small and dirty. It also stank of urine. It was dimly lighted by a
guttering candle set on the floor next to a figure wrapped in what
looked like a horse blanket.

Still holding on to me, Saunders kicked savagely at the

recumbent one until a wild-eyed man sat up and without a word crawled on all fours out of the room, dragging the blanket with him.

"Damn bastard," Saunders muttered as he picked up the candle and set it on an old wooden chair (the only article of furniture in the room). "If he comes back once more he won't be able to creep out of here."

"Let go of me, please," I begged. "My arm hurts."

"All right, but don't try to leave. Hear me? And for God's sake, stop crying. Make yourself at home," he said, laughing in an ugly way and pointing to a corner of the room. "Get over there and settle down, your ladyship, and be quiet. Go to sleep."

I have tried so hard for so long to forget the horrors of the Five Points that I'm not sure I have all the details straight. Even now, what I do remember clearly has the quality of a terrible nightmare from which I keep struggling to awaken.

He watched me go slowly over to the farthest corner of the room and slump down against the wall with the afghan wrapped around me, and I watched him stretch out in front of the closed door, presumably so that I'd have to climb over him if I tried to leave. How long I sat huddled in the corner staring at the flickering light of the candle I have no idea; I know that after a while I was so stiff and uncomfortable that I rolled myself up in the afghan and, using my good arm for a pillow, lay down on the hard, dirty floor. Just like the creature that crawled out of here, I thought. I couldn't see Saunders's face, but I sensed that he was watching me. He said nothing, however, and some time later, maybe minutes, maybe hours, I fell asleep.

The room was in total darkness when I woke up with a start. Someone was knocking, or banging, on the door, and when Saunders opened it I could see by the light in the hall a big man wearing a long black overcoat and a fur hat. He was carrying an oil lamp in one hand and what looked like a cudgel in the other, though I couldn't see it clearly.

"Two weeks' rent you owe me," he growled. "Hand it over. If I don't have that money tomorrow morning, you're evicted."

Saunders's reply was inaudible, and after some angry, threatening words the rent collector or landlord turned away. I struggled up and started toward the door shouting, "Help me, help me! I am a prisoner! Help me, please!" hoping he'd hear me, but if he did he probably thought I was one of the drunken wretches who lived in the building. In any case he didn't come back. No sooner were the words out of my mouth than I heard Saunders coming through the darkness toward me, and before I could cry out again he struck me such a wicked blow on the side of my head that I fell to the floor.

"Keep your mouth shut or you'll get worse than that," he said in a voice that seemed to come from a great distance, and after that, nothing. . . .

Chapter Sixteen

H a! Yer wakin' up, are yez?" a raspy woman's voice cried out as I struggled up to a sitting position. "He tole me ter watch, see that yer don't git off. Sez he'll pay me t'watch, he sez."

I ached all over, and the blow to my head had left me feeling dull, as if I didn't have all my wits about me. Besides, and of immediate importance, my bladder was uncomfortably full.

"I have to go use . . ." I muttered. "I must . . ."

"Over dere in a corner." The speaker, a slatternly woman who sat hunched over on the room's only chair warming her hands over a candle stuck in a bottle, pointed to a chamber pot almost hidden in the shadows. She leered at me, exposing a mouthful of broken, discolored teeth. If I hadn't felt so miserable, I think she would have frightened me.

"G'wan," she ordered. "He won't like it if ye wet yerself, now, will 'e?"

"Where did he go?" I asked when I finished using the filthy pot. "When will he be back?"

" 'Oo knows?" she answered. "Sez t'watch yez, no more."

I started for the door but hadn't managed more than two or three steps before I felt an extremely strong arm around my neck, almost choking me.

"Set down," she ordered, pushing me onto the chair she'd just left and then stationing herself in front of the door. "That's it. Now stay put. I wants me money. . . ."

"Listen," I said softly, "listen to me: I'll give you more money than he ever will if you come with me to my house."

" 'Ow do I know yer will?" she sneered. " 'Oo are ya?"

"I am Marike Bogardus, and my husband is a rich man. Come with me, and I will give you money and food, too."

Food! I thought, food! When had I last had anything to eat or drink?

"What time is it?" I asked the woman. "I'm hungry and thirsty."

"So's everybody," she said. "Mayhap he'll feed yer pies and whiskey."

"What time is it?" I asked again.

"Almost sunup, still dark out."

"Please, please let me out of here!" I cried in desperation. "Come with me! I promise I'll pay you and then you can buy yourself pies and drink."

"G'wan wit yer! Leave me man? No, missus. What'll happen to me without me man? He's not much to look at, but he brings me gin. Eh, lookee! 'Ere's yer own big fella! 'Ere's yer woman, mister, safe like yer said. Gimme me pay!"

"Get out, you dirty slut," Saunders growled, pushing the woman through the door. She was wiry, and resisted him, but he was so much stronger that she ended up in a heap out in the hall.

"Come with me, girl," he said, turning to me. "We must be there before."

"Before what?" I asked angrily. "And now where are you going to take me?"

"Before daylight, and you'll see where you're going when we get there. I've got too many people chasing me down to get paid. We can't stay here any longer. Come, stir yourself! Hurry up, or we'll be seen."

Who would see us at this hour, I wondered as we stepped around the miserable woman who'd been guarding me and made our way down those dangerous stairs and out into the cold dawn. Saunders took a firm grip on my arm again and started to walk at a good pace so that before long we had left the littered streets of the Five Points and were making slower progress through a field of stubble.

"I'm hungry," I said plaintively. "I'll faint if I don't eat something soon. Do you want me to die?"

"You won't die. You'd be no good to me dead. There's food and drink where we're going but only if you are careful to keep your mouth shut. No one is to know who you are or you really will wind up dead. Not far now."

I have read that one's memory can be faulty, that it can play tricks on a person, and perhaps mine has since I have tried unsuccessfully for so long a time to banish Hugh Saunders and everything connected with him from my mind. Maybe, though, by the time I've finished writing this account of his misdeeds and brutality his image will have faded away once and for all. I fervently hope so.

He pulled and dragged me along over the rough ground until I wrenched my ankle and fell, at which time he swore angrily and kicked me.

"Damn it, get up," he hissed, yanking my arm until I thought it would come off. "Get up, girl. Do you want to freeze to death?"

I made no answer. I could have told him that I was already half frozen and that a little more wouldn't matter, but suddenly he picked me up and threw me over his shoulder like a sack of flour. The afghan, which I still had wrapped around me, caught on something, a bramble or a thornbush, and the last thing I saw for a while was a small tangle of bright red yarn glowing in the early morning sun. Perhaps a bird will find it and line its nest with it, I thought, beginning to cry again.

"Shut up," commanded Saunders. "We're nearly there."

I could see that we had turned into a narrow street, really just an alley, and moments later he set me down in front of a small brick house, still keeping a firm hold on me while he banged on a heavy wooden door.

"Where is this?" I asked, leaning against him in order to take the weight off my aching ankle.

He made no reply, and moments later a tall woman wearing a long, shiny red dress opened the door and shouted: "Stop that racket! Don't you know better than to be wakin' people up at the crack of dawn? Oh, it's you, Hughie. Who's this with you? Someone come to be with my girls?"

"Right, Peg," he answered. "Just let us in and feed us something hot."

"She's some pretty, Hughie. Clean her up and put a satin dress on her and she'll do good for us."

"For God's sake, Peg, stop the talk."

"Yes, yes, I heard you, but where's what you're owin' me, Hughie boy?"

"You'll get it, Peg," he said, and then leaned so close to her that I couldn't hear their whispered conversation, but eventually the door was opened wide enough to allow us to step into a narrow but blessedly warm hall. When a smiling black woman almost completely enveloped in a large white apron opened a door at the back of the house, allowing the tantalizing smell of frying bacon to escape from the kitchen, the woman Peg beckoned to her.

"Josie, come," she commanded. "Take this young one into the back and clean her up and feed her before she faints. I'll take care of Mr. Hugh in the parlor."

"Yes ma'am, Miss Peg," the black woman responded. "Come on, young one," she said, putting an arm around my shoulders and guiding me along the hall. "That's it, honey, lean on me and you won't fall down. Here we are; you set, and Josie'll get you some nice hot soup."

She brought me a bowl of what I thought at the time was the best-tasting, most wonderful soup I'd ever had in my life. It was thick, with pieces of tender chicken, slivered carrots, tiny onions, and slices of potatoes, and although I have never been able to eat quickly, that day I did, and mopped the bowl with pieces of the homemade bread she gave me.

She watched me, smiling, and after setting a mug of tea and

a plate of bacon and eggs in front of me she sat down on the opposite side of the table.

"Eat it all, missy," she said. "Do you good."

"Thank you," I said. "I was so hungry . . ."

I couldn't go on; tears streamed down my cheeks and I all but choked on a morsel of bacon.

"No, now, missy, don't cry. You're goin' to be fine," she said soothingly, handing me a clean cloth to wipe my eyes. "That's it, try that tea. It'll make you feel better. Good tea it is. You don't get it just anywhere."

"It is good," I said a few moments later. "What kind is it? English tea?"

"Don't ask me, honey. Miss Peg gets it from the widder, and where it comes from I don't know."

She sighed and sat back in the chair, still watching me gravely.

"Where you come from, missy? Who tole you about Miss Peg?"

"I never heard of Miss Peg, Josie. I come from over on Beaver Street, where I live with my husband and children. That's where I was when . . ."

I stopped speaking abruptly when the kitchen door opened, and Miss Peg came in with Saunders right behind her. He held a tankard—of ale, I suppose—and stood looking down at me, murmuring something about my getting cleaned up. If I'd known how to put a sneering expression on my face I would have done so then, but the best I could do was to stare at him coldly.

"Yes indeed," Miss Peg was saying. "Take her inside, Josie, and fix her up. Find one of Cassie's gowns—that should about fit her—and then let her sleep so she'll be in shape for tonight. Go on, now! I'll feed Hughie boy in here."

"What did she mean, Josie, 'in shape for tonight?'" I asked when the black woman had taken off my cloak and begun to undo my dress. "Why are you taking off my clothes?"

"Got to wash you, honey. Fix you up."

"Why? I just want . . . What is this place? What happens to-night?"

"The men come, honey. You gotta look nice an'—"

"What men? I want to go home."

"Don' you know? This house is a house of pleasure for men, honey."

I was stunned. "You mean a brothel? I can't stay here, I can't—"

"Look, honey, I got your face and neck and arms all clean, an' now I'll fix your pretty hair real nice and then you can lay down and rest up."

I opened my mouth to scream, but before I could make a sound Josie clapped a fat, soft hand across my jaw and warned me to be quiet.

"You yell, honey, an' Miss Peg give you some beatin'. A big whip she got. Now be quiet, do, an' Josie'll come back soon."

I sat on the edge of the bed, clad only in my shift, and watched her leave. She closed the door firmly behind her, and a moment later I heard the sound of a key being turned in the lock.

It seemed immodest, improper, for me to sit there dressed only in my underwear, and when my eyes lighted on my old homespun morning dress that Josie had left draped over the back of a chair I got up and put it on. I also wrapped myself in my woolen cloak, which I found hanging on a hook near the window. Then, feeling warmer and more comfortable than I'd felt for hours and hours, I lay down on the bed and tried to think of a way to get out of a locked room. Perhaps something in the tea made me sleepy; Josie had said that Miss Peg had bought it from the widow. Did she mean the widow Riddell? I wondered. Was it some special herb? I didn't seem able to control my thoughts and found myself lazily watching the pale sunlight coming in through the barred window and wondering what time it was. After a while I fell into a deep, heavy sleep and did not wake up until a girl came into the room carrying a long green dress with spangles down the front of it.

"My name's Cassie," she said with a little smile. "You're to take off those clothes and put this on. I'll wait for you. If it fits we'll go inter the parler."

"What happens in the parlor?" I asked.

"We wait," she answered. "Wait till the men come."

"And then?" I persisted.

"Whaddya think? If one of 'em points to you, you go with him."

"Go where?"

"Where'd you think? To bed, o'course. Don't you know nothin'?"

"I can't put on that dress," I all but hissed at her, "and I am not going into any parlor. You go ahead."

Before I could say anything more the door was flung open, and an angry-looking Saunders stormed into the room. Cassie slipped out, dropping the spangled dress on the floor as Josie came in carrying a plate of food. She looked worried.

"She be all right, Mistah Hugh," she said, setting the plate down carefully on the small table next to the bed. "Gettin' dark out, an' we need a lamp if we're goin' to dress up. I'll stay here,

Mistah Hugh, if you go an' get one. Ask Miss Peg; she give it to you."

To my surprise he left the room without protesting, returning a few minutes later with a lighted oil lamp.

"No more delays, girl," he said roughly. "Be in the parlor in ten minutes or it will go ill with you." He gave a dark, threatening look and then left, slamming the door behind him.

I started to tell Josie that I would not wear the green dress for anything, but I stopped when I saw her put her finger to her lips. After listening at the closed door for a few moments she whispered softly that she would help me steal out the back way.

"You don't b'long here, honey," she said, shaking her head in disapproval. "An' Josie don' b'long here either. They only wants to make money off you. Jes' be quiet an' Josie'll get you away."

As she opened the door a crack to listen we both heard a tap, tap, tap at the barred window and turned to look. In the darkness I could see little, but I knew immediately—from the rhythm of the tap, perhaps—that Tanka was out there. Then I saw a finger beckon and point to the door of the bedroom. I nodded to the face I couldn't see and moved swiftly to where Josie stood, still with a finger to her lips.

Cheerful voices and sounds of revelry came from what I knew must be the parlor, and still Josie waited. Only when a loud burst of male laughter rang through the place did she move. She grabbed my hand and hustled me through the now-deserted kitchen into a narrow passageway and out into the dark, cold night.

Tanka, who was at my side in an instant, took my free hand and without a word led the two of us across a field strewn with rubble and boulders. After a while we passed a group of men, no more than three or four, sitting around a small fire and passing a bottle from one to the other. They paid us no attention, for which I was grateful, but I noticed that Tanka incensed his pace until we were well beyond the spot where they huddled.

"Where is this?" I asked. "Tanka, where?"

"Sh, sh," he whispered. "Not far now, Miss Ma. Home soon."

I should explain here that he had never been able to bring himself to call me Marike, although I had urged him to time and again. (He had no trouble with Philip's first name, though.) In the early days in Ossining he didn't call me anything at all, but after a while, when his English had improved, he heard Margretta's little voice saying "Ma, Ma" and decided on Miss Ma, which he used from then on.

What a good, kind man he was! He asked no questions about Josie (knowing instinctively, I think, that she was to be trusted), taking her arm when she stumbled and pausing when she seemed to be out of breath.

"Where's Philip?" I asked when we stopped to rest for a few moments.

"He looks for you, Miss Ma. I call him soon as we get home. Mr. Cutler stay with the little ones. See, we soon there."

He put a gentle arm around my shoulders as we emerged into the familiar streets of lower Manhattan and I began to cry again, this time with relief that the ordeal of the last two days was over.

Chapter Seventeen

I found myself smiling with pure happiness when I picked up my pen this morning to write about what happened after our arrival at Beaver Street. I can still almost feel the warmth of my children's arms around me and hear their tearful, joyful cries of welcome, but I must not linger over those memories. . . .

When Tanka, Josie, and I had crossed John Street the Indian began to whistle a series of birdcalls I remembered hearing in Ossining on summer afternoons.

"For Philip?" I asked.

"Yes, if he be not too far off. If so, I get you home safe and go find him. Maybe he hears me, though."

"Philip is your man?" Josie asked. "What will he think of Josie?"

"Don't worry," I said. "Yes, he's my husband, and a good man. He'll be grateful to you for helping me. Oh, oh! We're home!"

Those inside the house must have heard Tanka's whistles. Before we could raise the knocker the front door was opened by

Mr. Cutler with one hand while he used the other to keep Margretta and Adrien from running out. In no time both children were in my arms, hugging and kissing me and plying me with questions. I tried to put them down when Philip came in, but he ended up embracing all three of us, almost sobbing with relief that I was safe. Then suddenly we were all talking at once, but not for long. Mr. Cutler and Philip were too anxious to capture Saunders and, guided by Tanka, set out for Miss Peg's establishment without delay.

That Josie was worried about what was to become of her was evident from her troubled expression, but when I told her she could surely stay with us and that she could sleep in my brother Pieter's old room she smiled and asked me if she could go in the kitchen and cook us something to eat.

I was in bed and almost asleep when Philip and Tanka came back (Mr. Cutler went to his own lodging) with the news that Saunders had disappeared, owing money not only to Miss Peg but also to several of the men who were still in the parlor.

"We'll catch him sooner or later, love," Philip said as he slipped into bed beside me. "He obviously has no money, and—"

"Oh, but he is resourceful."

"Yes, but right now he's desperate. He apparently went wild when he realized you were gone. He tore through the brothel like a madman and then raced out of the place. You see, he expected the woman Peg to pay him well for bringing you there; he was counting on that money."

"How did Tanka find me? Tell me, Philip."

"Tomorrow, love. It's late. Come close to me—yes, kiss me."

"Philip was the one who saw the number five you scratched on the stone," Tanka said the next morning after Philip had left for the chandlery. "But he didn't understand right away. First he had to think about many number fives. But finally he figured it mean the Five Points, so we go there, go to many, many houses. Took time. Then we find one angry man, and when we say what Saunders look like he tells us he saw him, but he ran off with a girl and owed him money.

"We ask which way he went. The man don't know, but point over the fields, so Philip go one way and I go other way. I have no sign, no hope until I see this."

He put his hand into one of his many pockets and pulled out the ragged strands of red yarn I had last seen lying in a frozen field with the early sun shining on it.

"Then I knew, Miss Ma, where you'd been, and I had to find where you went."

As he told it, the story sounded like a careful search of the surrounding area. At first he went, maybe not inch by inch, but certainly very slowly, over the nearby ground, thinking I might have left another clue.

"What took me a long time," he said ruefully, "was no footprints showed. Ground too hard, too stony. I think and think. Then I see houses. Maybe you go there. I knock on doors, but people scream at me and say go away. Then I look in windows, many windows, and then I see you."

"The moment I heard you tapping, Tanka, I knew I'd be safe," I said, reaching out to take his hand. "But tell me, what will happen now? Saunders—"

"He go to ground someplace, Miss Ma. We find him. And now I go buy what you need and bring the water in. Then I go to the shop. Philip say you and little ones stay in house with Josie. Keep doors and windows locked and you be all right."

When Philip came home that night I remembered to ask him what Saunders had written in the note he'd left on the kitchen table. It was a demand for two hundred pounds, to be handed to him at midnight of the night I was taken at the corner of Broadway and Pine Streets.

"I was there with the money, Marike," Philip said, "hoping to see you—I was nearly frantic with worry—and waited and waited, but no one ever came. If it hadn't been for Tanka . . ."

Chapter Eighteen

T he next weeks passed slowly and uneventfully with no
news of Hugh Saunders. Philip and Tanka were busy at
the chandlery, but Mr. Cutler kept on with a fruitless
search. The constables and the night watch remained on the
lookout for the man, but there'd been no sign of him, and we all
began to think he'd left the city.

Josie settled into our house easily and comfortably, taking over
what I thought was more than her share of the daily chores. She
cleaned, polished, and scrubbed, she washed the clothes, and
would have done all the cooking had I permitted it. Philip was
delighted that at last I had some household help, but Anna was
not so pleased. One day when she visited me and saw Josie out
in the back garden unpegging the clothes from the line she
turned away from the window and sat down at the kitchen table
looking miserable.

"We used to have a slave, too," she whined.

"Josie is not a slave, Anna," I said quickly. "She was freed several years ago, and Philip pays her wages. She said she'd work for her room and board, but we didn't think that was right."

"Well, I could use someone like that, Marike, but of course Mama wouldn't allow it. She's *such* a trial, and just now . . ."

She broke off and stared down at the cup of tea I'd poured for her. An odd expression played on her face.

"Just now what, Anna? What were you about to say?"

"Oh, nothing. You know how difficult she can be. She wears me out, that's all. And even if we could find someone to do what Josie does, she wouldn't have her in the house."

"But she had Essie, your slave, for years."

"That was different. My father bought Essie so long ago—it was as if she'd always been there. Mama didn't know anything else then. And now, oh, I don't know, I don't know what to do."

She began to cry, but when she heard Josie at the back door she quickly wiped her eyes and said she'd better go.

"Josie," I said later on when I was washing up the tea things, "remember the tea you gave me to drink at Miss Peg's house? You said she got it from a widow."

"That's right," she said. "Yes, ma'am, from the widder."

"Could that have been the widow Riddell? I went to her house a few times to get a potion for Mrs. Bogardus."

"I don' know her name, honey. All I know is Miss Peg say to give it to all the new girls. Makes 'em sleepy, she says, so they be rested when the men come. Special tea, it was."

It's strange, I thought when I'd settled down in the front room to finally mend the torn corner of the afghan, strange that Anna has never said a word about what Hugh Saunders did to me. I know Philip told her about it; doesn't she believe him? Perhaps she doesn't want to believe it. . . . Poor Anna! Knowing what I do about that man I can't imagine that she'd ever be happy with him; but then, she's desperately unhappy without him.

She was still on my mind the next morning, which I had spent baking, and when I was taking two sweet-smelling dried-apple pies from the oven it occurred to me that the women in the Water Street house might relish their spicy flavor.

"Mm, mm, that smells good!" Josie exclaimed. "You a fine baker, honey."

"We won't need both of these tonight, Josie, even if Mr. Cutler comes for supper. If I wrap one of them up would you take it over to Miss Anna and her mother on Water Street?"

"Somethin' wrong in that house, Miss Marike," Josie said when she returned from delivering the pie. "That's one sick ole woman, an' Miss Anna, she so strange."

"What do you mean, Josie?"

"She keep lookin' aroun'—I dunno. Didn't even ask me to set down way you do. Somethin on 'er mind, like."

"Was the old lady sick in bed?"

"No, ma'am. She set in the parlor, wrapped up in shawls, big eyes starin' at me. Not sayin' nothin'. Can't she talk?"

"Yes indeed, she can talk. But what makes you think she's sick?"

"I know that look, Miss Marike," Josie said slowly. "I seen it before. She one sick woman."

I was not unduly worried about Mrs. Bogardus; she was not a woman apt to change her habits easily or relinquish her comfort, and too many times had I seen her sitting in silence, wrapped in her shawls, with the volume of Calvin on her lap. I was more concerned about Anna's welfare; Josie's remarks about her behavior reminded me of the strange expression that had crossed my sister-in-law's face, a sly or secretive look, when she said "Mama's such a trial, and *just now* . . . " Didn't her words indicate that something other than Mrs. Bogardus was upsetting her? Was she feeling poorly herself? I tried, but I couldn't think of any way to make her life easier, and Philip was of no help there. When I repeated Josie's comments to him later that evening he merely said his mother was acting as usual and that Anna was moping over Saunders's disappearance; he didn't know what could be done for either of them.

"If we could find Saunders," he mused, "and either put him in jail or let Cutler take him back to England (if he doesn't kill him first), then maybe Anna will stop dreaming about him. Other than that I just don't know. What I do know is that I hate going to that house these days. Oh, let's not talk about it anymore."

"Would you like a mug of cider, Philip?" I asked, thinking the hot drink might cheer him up. "It's good and spicy."

"Not just now, love," he answered, taking a roll of papers from his pouch and spreading them out on the table. "Come and look at these plans for a new house. I had John Pryor draw them up for us. He's a well-known architect; he designs houses for people with plenty of money. Do you realize that we've become really very well off? Maybe not exactly wealthy, but we have lots of money. The chandlery does well, but better than that are the profits from my investments in merchant shipping. We'll be able to afford a great house! Now sit down and see if you like this design; he's given us large rooms with plenty of big windows to let the daylight in. What do you think? Look, here's where our bedroom will be."

"Great news, Marike," Philip said one evening early in April. "I've bought some lots. Mr. Astor had them for sale up on Elizabeth Street, just the place for us! Now the building can begin. There'll be room for a garden, but it looks as there'll be no farm for us."

"That's just as well," I said. "I saw how hard Uncle Franz has to work at farming—not that you don't work hard, my dear husband."

"Yes, look at it this way," he said. "Let's say the farm was a boyhood dream, and best forgotten. I'm a city man, and I like being one."

"Did you see Anna today?" I asked, watching him take out the plans for the new house. "She hasn't been over here in weeks."

"No," he said slowly. "I've had no desire to go there. I see that their money is paid to them, but there's nothing else I can do."

"I think, Philip, that I'll pay her a visit tomorrow."

"Really, love? You know how my mother . . ."

"Yes, I know that she'll scream at the sight of me, but I *am* worried about Anna and want to see her. I thought I would go around to the kitchen door and then Mrs. Bogardus won't know I'm there. I could go in the afternoon when she's upstairs having her rest. Josie will be here when the children come home from school, so they'll be all right. Philip, I feel I must go; something may be wrong with Anna. She might be sick. Anyway, I feel that she'd be more apt to confide in me than she would in you."

In the end he agreed that I was probably right and said I might go if I promised not to stay too long. Accordingly, I set out the following afternoon, a lovely spring day it was, too, arriving at the Water Street house shortly before three o'clock. The place looked as unwelcoming as ever, with dark curtains drawn across the windows facing the street and dead leaves and bits of trash strewn about on the steps leading up to the front door. Another sign of the change in Anna, I thought; she used to be such a demon about sweeping and scrubbing those steps.

I walked quietly to the back of the house, and as I looked in through the kitchen window, the one over the sink, I saw, or thought I saw, the door leading to the cellar open and close, but the glass in the window was dirty, and I couldn't be sure. Perhaps it was just a shadow, or a reflection of some sort.

"No, the visit could not possibly be called a successful one," I said in answer to Philip's question that night. "Anna kept saying she was all right, but she did not look at all well. Her eyes were red, her skin had an unhealthy, sallow look, and she was terribly thin. And nervous! When she made tea for us she spilled hers on the table—you know that's not like her, not like her at all—and she held her head as if she was listening for her mother. She did try to be pleasant, asking about Margretta and Adrien, but it didn't sound natural, and I could see that it was an effort for her."

"Did you ask if she needed anything, Marike?"

"Yes, and she said no, nothing. But, Philip, something is wrong with her. She seemed to be worn out, and it can't be from too much hard work; the house is dusty, uncared for. Dishes were piled up in the sink and she had to take a bunch of unwashed pots off the table when we sat down to have the tea. Also, there was an empty bottle, a whiskey bottle, I think, in the corner. Do you think she's been drinking spirits?"

"I'll find out," he said grimly. "I'll go over there tomorrow. What did she say about my mother?"

"Just that she'd been fussing about the food and complaining about everything."

"Well," he said after a few minutes' thought, "the first thing I'll do will be to find someone to clean the place up. This can't go on."

Later, after Philip had gone to sleep, I was wakeful and restless, unable to put the strangeness of my visit out of my mind. All at once, as if a light suddenly came on in a dark room, I understood what was wrong: I knew that I *had* seen the cellar door open and close, and that it had closed on Hugh Saunders.

Chapter Nineteen

A re you sure Saunders is there, Marike?" Philip asked the next morning. "Did you see him?"

"No, I didn't, but everything points to him. Philip, I *know* he's there; I *know* Anna's been hiding him."

I could see that Philip was not convinced, and I was at a loss to explain why I was so sure of what I said. He frowned, and waited a minute or two before speaking.

"Why is she so unhappy then? If she's so mad about him and has him with her—I don't understand—but I'll go and see. First, I'll get hold of Cutler; this might be his chance to catch Saunders. We'll go at once. Come on, Tanka."

I knew Philip wouldn't let me go with them, so I didn't bother to ask. I busied myself in the kitchen, a better way to pass the time until I heard from him than just sitting and wondering. I did not have to wait long: scarcely an hour had passed when Tanka returned with the news that Anna was not in the house. She had left a note saying she was going away with Hugh Saunders and that no one was to try to find them.

"But her mother, Tanka; did she leave her there all alone?"

"The old lady dead, Miss Ma," he answered. "Philip say for you to come."

"You were right, love," Philip said when Tanka and I arrived at the Bogardus home. "Saunders was here, right under our noses the whole time. Cutler's wild; I don't know when I've seen anyone so angry. He's gone off to alert the constables and to try to figure out where they're headed."

"Is your mother in her bed?" I asked. "Did she die in her sleep?"

"She may have died while she was sleeping, yes, but she's in the front room. You don't have to see her if you don't want to; she may have died in her sleep, but it seems she was having nightmare. In fact, I'd like you to go over the rest of the house with me and see if we can find any clues, anything pointing to where Anna and Saunders might be going. Cutler is determined to go after them, and I'll send Tanka with him if we can just find out where."

We found nothing helpful except that Anna had taken all the warm clothes she owned, which seemed strange, since summer was coming on.

"They must be headed north," I said, picking up an old gingham dress that had fallen to the floor. "Canada, maybe. Remember, Saunders is British, and he might feel safer there."

Tanka agreed with me and was ready to go after them at once. "I go, Philip," he said excitedly. "I pick up their trail."

"No, Tanka," Philip said firmly. "Look, there's no money in the house; they took it all, as well as my mother's jewelry, so they are not going by foot. Probably they took a stagecoach, or they could have sailed. You'd be wasting your time, Tanka. We'd do better to wait; Saunders will get into trouble, and we'll hear then."

As I looked down at the pathetically fragile, almost childlike figure still wrapped in her shawls, huddled in the large armchair next to the fireplace, I wondered how I could ever have been afraid of her. Then I went closer and saw her mouth distorted in a frightful grimace and nearly cried out. Had she died in unbearable pain? I asked myself. Had she been trying to call for help? A frantic call that was never answered?

I'd had little experience with death until then, but it was obvious to me that my mother-in-law's had not been a peaceful departure from this life. Her expression was one of terror. Her eyes were staring—at what?—at whom? Her mouth was open as if in one last, terrified scream, the hands clenched on the arms of the old, worn fabric of her favorite chair, all signifying either violence or helpless fear.

As I turned to leave the poor woman in the dusty gloom of the room in which she had spent so many of her days, I caught sight of the pewter cup lying on the floor near the chair, the one from which she always drank her potion. It had evidently slipped from her hand just as she was seized with pain or panic.

When I picked it up I noticed at once that although it was empty a strong, strange smell clung to it, not the rather pleasant scent of rum and lemon I had come to associate with her potion, but something else that I didn't recognize. I stood quietly for a few minutes, turning the cup around in my hands, admiring the delicate tracery of grapevines on the body of it and the intricate border of tiny leaves at the top. Would the widow Riddell know what that smell came from? I wondered. If so, she could tell me what was in that last potion.

Philip called me at that moment, and after wrapping the cup in a napkin that had been left on the small table next to the old lady's chair, I slipped it into my pocket before going back into the kitchen. I ought to have gone immediately to the widow's house, but somehow I didn't want to hear that what I smelled was poison.

Mrs. Bogardus had made a will leaving the Water Street house to Philip (I thought his father had left it to him, but his mother evidently thought it was hers), with the stipulation that he never bring his wife, Marike, to live in it with him. To Anna she bequeathed her silver, her jewelry, and whatever household articles she wanted. Little did she know that nothing of value was left. Anna and Hugh Saunders had either sold or taken with them anything that was worth money. The Water Street house was nothing but an empty shell.

As the weeks went by and the balmy spring weather gave way to the baking heat of summer we thought less and less about the runaways, assuming that by that time they were beyond our reach.

"Maybe we've seen the end of them," Philip said. "I certainly hope so. I feel sorry for poor Cutler, though. He's begun to talk about giving up the search and going back to England. I think he's worried about his daughter. Anyway, I am through with Anna and Saunders; other things are more important."

He had sold the Water Street house, saying he never wanted to see or hear of it again, and invested the money in more of the merchant ships that were doing a brisk trade with some of the South American countries. Since we were both busy watching and supervising the building of our house on Elizabeth Street and making plans for furnishing it, I was not too anxious to leave the city that summer. There'd been, however, something strange, almost pleading in Tante Greta's last letter, begging me to bring the children to Ossining for the hot weather. "And make Tanka come, too," she wrote. "Franz needs him to help with the crops."

"That doesn't sound like Tante Greta, or like Uncle Franz, either," I said to Philip. "There must be something wrong. I think I'd better go; they've been so good to me and never asked for anything in return."

"It's probably just that they're getting on in years, love," he said. "I agree, though, that it would be a good thing if you went. I can spare Tanka for a couple of weeks, and he'd like the trip, I know."

The Hudson valley was not noticeably cooler than the city we'd left behind, but the deep shade cast by the huge old trees in the lane leading to the farmhouse provided a welcome change from the heat of the sun. Uncle Franz met us with one of his wagons where the stage let us out in Ossining village, and while I thought he looked tired he seemed cheerful enough and obviously delighted that Tanka had come.

"Wonderful fruit this year, Tanka," he said. "Big crop, big.

Peaches, many, many peaches, and early apples, good apples, and of course, your favorites—the pears, ready to harvest. Some will come later, too, but they can wait."

"We pick them," Tanka responded. "Adrien help. Pile them in baskets. Good boy, Adrien. Margretta help, too."

My uncle may have been short of help, but I soon realized that that was not his reason for wanting the Indian to come with us.

"He worries, Marike," Tante Greta said when she and I were alone in the kitchen. "That man, Saunders, Franz is worried he will return."

"Saunders!" I exclaimed. "Did you say 'Saunders'? Tante Greta, was Hugh Saunders here? Why? How did that happen?"

"Why, your sister brought him."

"Anna brought him here?"

"*Ja*, Anna. She said you told her to come here, that he would work for Franz."

"Tante Greta, I never did . . ."

"That's what she said. And they stayed and stayed and ate and drank. They didn't do much work."

"She is not my sister, but my sister-in-law, and the constables in New York are looking for him. He is a rascal and a thief. Where are they now?"

"Gone away. When I said you were coming, Marike, they whispered, and one morning I wake up and they are gone. Also gone is the money in the teapot, the one for show on the shelf. It was not so much money, but still."

Chapter Twenty

According to my uncle, Anna and Saunders had left the farm four days before our arrival.

"Perhaps they took the Albany stage," he said at supper that night. "Or maybe they go on foot. I do not know. That Saunders!" He shook his head in exasperation and took a sip of cider before continuing. "He is not a good man. He is lazy; he stole my grog, and when I caught him at it he say, 'What do you do about it?' "

"He is not good to Anna, either," Tante Greta said. "Why does she marry such a man?"

"They cannot be married," I said. "He has a wife in England, and her father is here in America looking for him."

"A criminal!" exclaimed my uncle. "I am right to be afraid of him. He might do anything, do us harm. Tanka, we need you to protect us. Your bow and arrows still stay in the barn, and I have my gun."

"Tomorrow I see if I find any trails," Tanka said. "Maybe they not too far away."

"What will you do if you find them?" I asked.

"I tie him up." Here Tanka made imaginary knots in the air with his long strong fingers. "I bring him back, give him to Mr. Cutler. Miss Anna, I do not know."

"I not know how long it takes, Miss Ma," Tanka said the next morning when I was putting together a package of food for him. "Maybe two, three, four days, maybe weeks. But I come back. Keep little ones close by and lock doors at night."

"They may be traveling by stagecoach, Tanka."

"I think they not, Miss Ma. Afraid someone see them. More likely they take boat across Hudson and head for Catskills. Not so many people in mountains. I look."

He was in a hurry to be off, still young enough to delight in the thought of adventure without worrying about the possible dangers involved. He'd become part of our family by that time, one of us, and it was with an uneasy mind that I watched him disappear swiftly and silently into the woods to the north of the farm. Then, to keep from worrying about him, I turned and began the preparations for breakfast.

The waiting was hard; every sound that could not be easily identified worried us, and even the children seemed to be on edge. I was beginning to wish I had left them in the city with Josie when we suddenly had word from Tanka. He'd been gone for almost a week when a trapper, Diedrich Brewer, an acquaintance of my uncle's, stopped by with the news that the couple had been seen in a small village above Kingston.

"Not much of a place, either," Brewer said. "Only eight or ten houses as far as I could see, a general store and a tavern. Funny name for a village, too; it's called Liza's Rock. It seems there was once an old woman, Liza, who'd come and sit for days at a time on a great rock alongside a waterfall at the edge of the forest. The story was that she had second sight and was able to cast spells, but who knows? She's long gone, but the tavern owner said some folks nonetheless claim to see her sitting there on the rock when there's a full moon.

"But you want to hear about Tanka; nice fellow, that Indian. I like him. I'd been out in the woods for a fortnight trapping beaver and squirrel—I send the skins to Jake Astor in New York—and was ready to come home. I'd made camp near Liza's Rock when Tanka showed up, and we talked. I'd just been into the general store for a few supplies and stopped at the tavern for a drink, and that's where I saw this couple. I couldn't get a good look at the woman because she kept her head turned away, but the man was a big, surly fellow—I'm sure he was the one your Indian looked for. He was speaking low to the girl and I could hear only a few words, something about a place to sleep, and— oh, yes, money. If they needed money why was he spending what they had on whiskey?"

"Did they have any baggage with them?" I asked.

"Not much," he answered. "All I saw was a cloth bag on the floor. The girl kept her hand on it."

"My laundry bag!" Tante Greta cried. "That's where it went. They put their clothes in it."

"What was Tanka going to do?" my uncle asked.

"Didn't say," replied the trapper, "but he said to tell you he'd get news to you somehow. He did say he thought the couple had

153

taken the stage until their money ran out and would have to go wherever they were headed on foot. Where? Who can tell?"

Poor Anna, I thought after Diedrich Brewer had left us. I don't really like you, Anna, but I have to wonder whether you deserve the hardships that have come your way; first your mother, then Saunders. Is it fair? Have we been fair to you, Anna?

Ten days after Diedrich Brewer's visit Mr. Cutler appeared at the farmhouse, bearing a letter for me from Philip. I have kept it all these years, folded safely away in a drawer to which I alone have the key. I reread it this morning, and have decided to include it here:

My dearest love, my only love,

I was happy to receive your letter and sad that you yourself did not come instead. When I told Mr. Cutler about Tanka's search for Saunders and Anna and how they were seen in a tavern in Liza's Rock, nothing would do but that he go after them, too. He will stop at Ossining first to be informed of any later developments and then go on. The man is beside himself with anger and the desire for revenge. What he will do to Saunders when he finds him I do not dare to think.

I wish I could come to you, but with Tanka away I dare not leave the chandlery. So, you must come to your poor, lonesome husband as soon as you possibly can, my dear one.

—Philip

Mr. Cutler wasted no time at the farmhouse. Tante Greta fed him a hearty meal, after which Uncle Franz drove him in the wagon to the Red Coach Inn, from which he could catch the stage going north.

My uncle did not think the Englishman would be of much help to Tanka. "He does not know the woods or the mountains," he said. "How could he? I just hope he does not get in the way of Tanka."

"His clothes, oh, those clothes," Tante Greta chimed in. "They are not for being in the forest."

I had to agree with her; he certainly was not dressed for life in the wilderness. He was wearing his expensive city clothing— fawn-colored trousers, a yellow waistcoat over a white cambric shirt, the whole surmounted by a fitted jacket with what we called "swallow tails" in the back. I hated to think how uncomfortably hot his fine clothing would make him feel once he was forced to travel on foot. Oh, and his feet! The shiny leather shoes he always wore were never meant for the rough trails. I was sure he would have sore, blistered feet in no time at all. Perhaps his anger at Saunders would sustain him.

Chapter Twenty-one

Toward dusk a few days after Mr. Cutler's departure, a steady rain was falling, a good soaking rain, as my uncle was describing it, just when a farmer drove his wagon around to the back of the farmhouse. Moments later he was at the kitchen door, carrying a blanket-wrapped bundle in his arms.

" 'Tis Anna!" exclaimed Tante Greta, pulling aside a corner of the blanket. "Your sister-in-law, Anna, Marike!"

"I found her sitting at the side of the road," the farmer said, shaking the water from his hat. "Crying, she was. She look bad. Said she live at Dykeman's farm. I wrap her in blanket and bring her."

She did look bad, poor, bedraggled Anna! Her thin, tear-stained face was streaked with dirt, and her familiar brown homespun dress was in tatters. She moaned, pitiful little sounds, but made no attempt to speak. Was she sick, I wondered, or in a swoon? We didn't know, and when Tante Greta and I had stripped off her wet clothes and washed her with warm water she still didn't move. We took turns sitting by her, rubbing her cold hands and speaking softly to her. My aunt brought in a bowl of soup, but no matter how I tried I could not get her to take a mouthful.

"She is too sick," Tante Greta said. "I fear she will die."

But Anna did not die; she slept all that night, the sleep of complete exhaustion, and did not wake up until noon of the following day. At first she was reluctant to tell us what had happened to her, but that evening, after Margretta and Adrien were in bed, she began to talk.

"In the beginning it wasn't so bad," she said, staring down at the folded hands in her lap. "We were lucky, I guess. We'd walk a little way and then manage to get a ride in a wagon—people were good to us—and then we'd stop at a lodging house and at least have a bed to sleep in, but then, oh, it got so bad. We had to walk and walk, walk so far that my shoes broke, and my feet hurt me so much."

"Where were you and Saunders going, Anna?" I asked.

"I don't know," she said despairingly. "He said one place and then another. First he said Albany, that there was a man there he knew, an Englishman, who would take care of us. Then he said no, we'd go to Canada, and then he said maybe Australia. He kept changing his mind, and he was so cross! I had to stop asking if we could stop and rest—I was so tired. I was afraid he'd hit me. And I was scared; the woods were so deep and it was getting dark. He said the trail would lead us out of the forest, but it didn't, and and just when I thought I was going to faint we came to a clearing with a big hole in it. I almost fell into it, and there was a little hut. Nobody lived in it, and Hugh said we'd sleep there."

"You had some food with you?" asked Tante Greta.

158

"Bread," Anna answered with a shudder. "Hard, stale bread, and he got water from a stream. That's all we had. There was nothing in the hut, no sign that anyone lived there."

"Must have belonged to the charcoal burners," Uncle Franz said. "You told us there was a clearing, yes? Well, when they'd used all the trees they needed there, they'd move on, sell the charcoal, find another spot, build another hut, and after a while leave that one, too. The hole you saw, that's where they charred the wood."

"It was awful," Anna continued. "At least we weren't out in the open in the night with all the wild animals, but we had to sleep on the hard ground. I was still scared and didn't want to close my eyes, but I was so tired I fell asleep, and when I woke up it was getting light and Hugh was gone."

"I waited. I thought he went for more water, but he never came back. He's gone, gone forever, Marike."

"And a good thing, too," Uncle Franz said softly. "And, Anna, you found your way back here?"

"Yes, I didn't know where else to go. I picked some blackberries and blueberries and drank some water from the stream. Then I walked back down the trail we'd followed for so long! Later, hours later, I came to a road. It was raining then, but I had to rest. I feared I'd fall down if I didn't. And then the farmer came by, a kind man . . ."

Her voice trailed off, and she closed her eyes for a moment or two. I thought she was falling asleep again, but suddenly her eyes flew open and she sat up straight.

"I must go back to the city, to Water Street. Hugh might go there. He did before. He knows I'll take care of him," she said, staring wildly around the kitchen, almost like an animal search-

159

ing for a means of escape. She sprang up from the rocking chair and would have run out the back door if my uncle hadn't caught her in his arms and held her until she stopped struggling.

"She is still in love with him," murmured Tante Greta. "She is mad, mad."

Maybe it is madness, I thought, or maybe it's something as simple as exhaustion and just looks like madness.

It took a good deal of coaxing before we eventually settled Anna in her bed, but that was only the beginning of a bad night for me.

"Stay with me, Marike," she begged. "I am afraid to be by myself. I do not know why. Please stay! Sleep here with me, then I will be safe. If you go away who knows what might happen? Oh, stay, please stay, or I will see evil things."

What could I do? If I didn't stay she might keep the entire household awake. Maybe I could lull her to sleep, I thought. I tried speaking softly to her, using the voice that had so often been successful with my children when they were wakeful, but it didn't work with Anna. She wanted to do the talking and rambled on for hours, repeating what she'd already said downstairs, adding a few details, and constantly speaking of Saunders. At times she praised him lavishly, commenting on his good looks, his lovemaking, his generosity, and then without warning she'd accuse him of being deceitful, unfaithful, or cruel.

"I could have killed him, Marike," she said in a voice so low that it was almost a whisper. "Many times I thought I would, and then he'd come to me and be so loving—oh, yes, many times I thought of killing him. It isn't hard to kill someone, you know."

I pretended to be asleep, hoping that my silence would make her stop talking. It evidently did, because in a little while she was quiet, and her even breathing told me that the poor distraught woman finally slept. But for a long while after that I was unable to stop thinking of her last remark: "It isn't hard to kill someone, you know."

Chapter Twenty-two

I wrote to Philip at length, relating Anna's story in detail, asking what he thought we should do with her and whether or not to tell her about the sale of the Water Street house.

She kept talking about returning to it, fixing it up with new curtains in the front room instead of the old dark draperies, new crockery in the kitchen, and even vases of fresh flowers on the mantelpiece. She probably saw herself and Hugh Saunders living there, happily settled, and I hadn't the courage to tell her that the house that had been her home for so many years was now owned by strangers. It would only upset her to hear that, I decided, and destroy the peaceful state of mind she was enjoying.

Tanka must have sensed that all was not well with Anna, for when he reappeared about a week after her return he took one look at her and merely smiled, then he nodded to us, which I took to mean that his mission had been successful. He chatted quietly with us about the crops and the weather, and waited until she went up to bed before he began his tale.

"Did Mr. Cutler find you?" my uncle asked as soon as we heard the door to the bedroom close.

"I find him," Tanka answered. "He surprise me, too. Mr. Cutler is a good man. He do everything I say. I see him before he sees me. He is sitting on bank, washing his feet. His shoes no good for walking in woods."

From the way Tanka told it I gathered that Mr. Cutler had not been quite the hindrance my uncle had feared. Tanka praised his "strong spirit" and commented on the Englishman's lack of complaints.

"He never say he too hot, too cold, or that he want to eat. I kill rabbits, sometimes birds; we cook them, eat them, catch fish, pick berries. Only one time he say he think of your pies, Miss Ma."

"But where did you find Saunders?" Uncle Franz asked impatiently. "I take it you did . . ."

"Every day I send Cutler on a short, easy path and I circle around a longer path. At night I meet him and we spend night together. Finally we catch up with Saunders. We find him. Three, four, maybe five days after I see Mr. Cutler we meet two Mohawks. I not know them, but they say which way they see a man go. I not know if it is Saunders, but it sound like him. Big fellow, they say, beard. It gets late, night coming, time to make camp, but we do not stop. I smell smoke, and there we find him putting wood on fire."

"What did he do when he saw you?" I asked.

"He run," Tanka answered. "We run. I catch him, pull him down. Strong man. He break away, run through woods. I think we lose him, but in dark place he does not see the gully and falls down in it. All stones there. He does not move. I think he hit his head. We climb down, tie him up and wait for day to come. He opens his eyes, he shouts at us. Mr. Cutler laughs."

"Where are Saunders and Cutler now?" Uncle Franz asked.

"They go to New York. We take Saunders to place where Mr. Cutler hire cart and driver, and say he take him to New York to see Philip and then on ship to jail in England. So I come here."

"What do we say to Anna?" Tante Greta asked, looking worried.

"Nothing," my uncle said severely. "Say nothing and she will forget him."

I knew from my aunt's expression that she didn't agree with him any more than I did, but I kept quiet.

By the time Anna, Tanka, the children, and I arrived at Beaver Street I was almost at my wits' end with Anna's jabbering and wild talk about how she was going to fix up her house. She never mentioned her mother as though she'd forgotten that she'd left her there. My head was aching, and I didn't want to think about how we were going to manage. Philip had written to me at Ossining saying he would take care of Anna, but he did not say how or where.

I soon realized that he didn't really know himself what to do with her, especially after the scene she made when she learned that her old home had been sold. When she screamed at both of us, calling us a mean, thieving pair of liars, Philip took her by the shoulders and shook her, hard. That wasn't like him at all.

"Now look here, Anna," he said angrily. "That house was

mine, not yours, to do what I liked with. Besides, you left it and went off with Saunders, taking everything of value with you. That's stealing, Anna, and makes you a thief."

"Hugh made me do it," she said, beginning to cry. "I didn't want to."

"But you did, didn't you? And you sold those things for whatever you could get. And you left your mother there to die."

"Hugh needed the money for whiskey," she wailed. "And Mama was old. She's better off . . ."

"Now listen to me," Philip shouted. "You will stay here until we find you a room in a boardinghouse where—"

"A boardinghouse!" she shrieked. "A boardinghouse where I'd be among strangers? No, no, Philip. I have no money, no clothes—how can I go among strangers?"

"I will find clothes for you, Anna," I said. "Some of mine will fit you, and I'll sew you some new ones."

"I don't want your clothes," she almost spat at me. "Where are my own? Philip, did you sell them with the house?"

"You took your warm clothes with you, Anna. You must have left them someplace. There were just a few old summer things on the floor."

"Oh, yes," she said more quietly, looking away from us. "Hugh was angry that day. He said I looked slovenly, like a streetwalker, and then he tore up some of my things. He couldn't help it, though. He didn't mean it; he was just so worried, so upset. Where is he, Philip? I want to see him. I heard someone say he was in the city."

"You can't see him," Philip answered shortly. "He's in jail, over in the Fields."

"In the jail!" she exclaimed. "Why? He never did anything wrong."

"Indeed he did, Anna. He snatched Marike out of this house and forced her into a brothel. That's a crime; it's called kidnapping, and he is being punished for that, among other things. He's in a cell with nothing in it, not even a pallet to lie on, and it serves him right. Later he will be taken to England, where he's wanted for theft and forgery. Cutler has arranged all that with the British and American authorities. You will never see him again, Anna, and you might as well get used to the idea. Now go to bed, for God's sake, and let us have some peace and quiet."

She looked rebellious for a moment or two, and then the vague expression I had seen before came over her face, and I knew she had put out of her mind everything Philip had said and was once more picturing life with Saunders.

We kept Anna with us at Beaver Street, and although it made for a crowded household we managed, mainly because of Josie's unfailing help. She took almost complete control of Anna, keeping her occupied with small chores and seeing that she never left the house by herself.

"She apt to run off," Josie said to me, "an' then where'd she go? I watch, an' she be safe."

Philip was anxious to get his sister out of the house and asked me to see if I could find a suitable boardinghouse. "I don't care what it costs, Marike," he said. "Just be sure it's a nice place, and maybe she'll be happy there."

I found what I thought were comfortable rooms at Mrs.

Beales's house, a pleasant sitting room overlooking Maiden Lane and a smaller but perfectly adequate bedroom next to it. The furnishings, while not new, were in good condition, and Anna could add whatever she pleased in the way of personal belongings and decorations. The dining room, two floors below, looked inviting, with places set for ten at the large round table and crimson drapes that could be drawn over the net curtains at the windows.

"Lodgers have breakfast and dinner here, ma'am," the landlady said after I had complimented her on the appearance of the room. "And some of them keep biscuits and fruit in their rooms. I don't allow any cooking upstairs, no making toast in the fireplace, not since old Miss Putney nearly set herself on fire. No sir, no sir."

"And your price, Mrs. Beales?"

"Four dollars a week, ma'am, for them two rooms. Reasonable enough, I say," she answered promptly.

Philip wouldn't object to paying that, I thought. He'd pay almost anything to have the house to himself again, so I gave Mrs. Beales two dollars to hold the rooms for us and said I would bring my sister-in-law over to see them the next day.

To my surprise Anna not only agreed to look at the rooms but also acted politely, even demurely, when I introduced her to Mrs. Beales. She who had been so totally set against the prospect of living in a boardinghouse had reversed herself so completely that I was puzzled, and while I was grateful for her change of mind I could not help but be a bit suspicious. This ladylike behavior made me wonder if she wasn't making plans to see Saunders. Perhaps she had fantasies of trying to free him from the prison cell in which he languished.

Philip said I was silly to entertain such wild ideas, and to please him I let the matter rest. In any case, I had far more pleasant things on my mind: the house on Elizabeth Street was nearing completion, and decisions about the placement of shelves, the type of paneling, the length of the mantelpiece, things like that, were up to me. I loved doing it and couldn't wait until I saw everything finished and all the furniture in place. I even made a little diagram of where the beds and chests were to go so that the rooms wouldn't look cluttered. There was plenty of space—at times I felt that I was literally squandering space—a delightful feeling after living for so long in crowded quarters. It was a happy time for me, but all too short: Philip, Tanka, the children, and I were finishing our evening meal on a Monday night exactly two weeks after Anna's departure for the boarding-house when we heard a loud rapping on the front door. Moments later Philip ushered into the kitchen an irate, red-faced man with a strong grip on one of Anna's arms.

"Take her back," he cried. "Keep her here or put her in the asylum! My wife's near crazy with her goings on! And—"

"All right, Mr. Beales," Philip interrupted. "We'll see that she gives you no more trouble. Come, Anna, sit down. No, over here."

"I take care of her, Mr. Philip," Josie said, putting an arm around Anna's shoulders. "Come with Josie, Miss Anna. We have a nice cup of tea. You want some cake?"

Tanka, Philip, and Mr. Beales followed me into the front room, where my two wide-eyed children huddled close to me.

"Is Aunt Anna sick?" Margretta asked in a frightened voice.

"She upset, little one," Tanka said before I could answer her. "She be better soon."

"Upset!" Mr. Beales almost howled. "She upset the whole house, screaming and crying all night, keeping the whole house awake. We need our sleep, and who can sleep with that ruckus going on? And at meals—no peace there, either. Not with her pushing her food aside, onto the floor, too. Broke two plates, she did. My wife won't have it."

"What do I owe you for the plates, Mr. Beales?" Philip asked. "What price do you put on them?"

"Five dollars would cover everything, sir, the mess she made in her rooms and all," Mr. Beales said more quietly, and a few minutes later he left, only slightly mollified. In the meantime Josie had taken Anna upstairs; I could hear her singing softly to her as I was putting the children to bed and had to marvel at the seemingly inexhaustible patience and compassion of that good woman.

"I can't put her in the asylum, Marike," Philip said, looking worried. "And I have no idea what to do with her. There must be something we can do to help her."

"No, we can't put her in the asylum with all those lunatics and drunkards; it would be like sentencing her to her death. We'll have to keep her, Philip. You once said that in the new house we'd have much more room, remember, and that she could live with us."

"So I did, love, but she'll still be a burden."

"Not if we could find someone, maybe a nursemaid, to look after her, be with her night and day. Could we afford that? And still keep Josie?"

"Of course we can, my love. We can afford all kinds of things nowadays. It will just be a question of finding someone who will put up with Anna. Maybe Josie will know someone."

Chapter Twenty-three

All through the winter of 1788 an epidemic of yellow fever raged in New York, and we were urged to stay in our homes as much as possible. It was a trying time for all of us, especially for the children, who missed their friends, their outdoor play, and visits to the chandlery. Anna, of course, demanded constant attention, and without Josie's help I think I might have gone mad. One bright spot, however, in that long, dull winter, was Mr. Cutler's news from England.

He wrote a long letter to Philip in which he thanked us both profusely for our hospitality while he was here and begged to be remembered to Tanka and "your kind relatives in the town of Ossining," but the most important item dealt with Saunders.

"I saw to it," Mr. Cutler wrote, "that he was escorted by the governor of the prison himself and two guards aboard the British ship *Arthurian*, where he was immediately secured in the brig. The third day at sea we ran into heavy weather, enormous waves and gale winds. I was not comfortable at all, and neither was anyone else on board.

"No one is quite sure how it happened, but since the cargo consisted mainly of kegs of molasses, heavy wooden crates containing cotton, sugar, and furs, as well as barrels of God knows what, several of which were careening around in the hold, the theory is that one or more of them crashed into the door of the brig and sprung the lock.

"In any event, Saunders got loose and made for the deck—I don't know where he thought he'd go. There two seamen tackled him and wrestled him down. Saunders fought hard, got to his feet again, ready to take on the two of them, when a surge in the storm knocked off part of a mast. It fell on Saunders, a big, heavy tree trunk, killing him instantly. His body now lies in the depths of the Atlantic, and although I had set my heart on seeing him hanged in England I am glad that it is all over.

"I am home now and happy to tell you that my daughter Charlotte is a changed person. I found her cheerfully painting landscapes (some of them very nice, indeed) and anxious to have me meet a young man who has been calling on her. When I told her about Saunders's end she said she couldn't imagine why she'd even paid the slightest attention to him, and that she wouldn't even say one prayer for 'his deceitful soul' (her words).

"I have not recovered the portrait of my dear wife, nor, of course, the funds that Saunders stole, but I have my daughter safe and sound, for which I am heartily grateful.

"Again I extend my heartfelt thanks to you and your good lady and remain Yr Obedient Servant, Edward Cutler."

Because of the rampant fever and the extreme cold that year everything in New York seemed to slow down, including the finishing of our new home. It was not, therefore, until the spring of 1789 that we were able to move into it, a few days after we had seen General Washington inaugurated as the first president of our nation on the balcony of the Federal Hall on Wall Street.

It was said that the great man left his Virginia home, Mount Vernon, reluctantly, which I believed when Philip told me that Washington was quoted as saying, "My movement to government will be accompanied by feelings not unlike those of a culprit who is going to his execution." He established himself, however, at number three Cherry Street, at the intersection of Cherry and Franklin, and for a while at least our city was the capital of the country.

"Are you sure he said that, Philip? It doesn't sound like the man who led the fight for our independence."

"Pretty sure," he answered me, "but who knows? Someone may have misheard him or just made it up. The general was never afraid of anything as far as I know."

If it had not been for the move from the Beaver Street house to the more elegant one on Elizabeth Street, with all the packing and unpacking it involved, I don't know when, if ever, I would have found out what had actually happened on two separate occasions in the past. As it was, I was almost too late to uncover the truth. I have never told anyone what I am about to write here, and perhaps I never will, but I must put it down on paper.

Tanka had taken the children to Ossining to spend most of the summer with my aunt and uncle so that I could devote myself to setting our new home in order. The household was running fairly smoothly, although our plan to hire a nursemaid for Anna did not work. She would have no one but Josie and threw such a terrible tantrum when I brought in a cheerful, middle-aged woman who'd had a position as a companion to an elderly widow that I was embarrassed. The woman, I forget her name, left in a huff, saying she wouldn't stay with Anna for any amount of money. In the end we found an Irish girl, Maggie Moran, to do the cleaning and whatever else Josie wanted her to do. Anna had no use for Maggie, either, and had to be coaxed and bribed to come out of her bedroom so that the girl could clean it.

I had time that summer to attend to things I'd been putting off for weeks, things that hadn't demanded my immediate attention. I began by going through the children's winter clothing, putting aside those they'd outgrown to give to Josie to take to a poor family she knew. Then I made a list of the replacements Margretta and Adrien would need in the fall and took it into my room to see if I had any material in the pine chest that would be suitable for dresses and shirts.

Underneath some of my own winter clothes I found a few lengths of flannel and muslin, and down near the bottom of the chest, underneath everything, I spotted an old green-and-gray striped skirt of mine, rolled up in an untidy ball.

"I never liked this skirt," I said aloud, holding it up to shake out the wrinkles. "Why did I keep it? I wonder. *Ow!*"

Something banged against my knee, and even before I looked in the pocket of the skirt I knew what it was. The little pewter cup I'd picked up from the rug in the Water Street house the day we found Mrs. Bogardus's body was still in the napkin I'd wrapped around it. It still retained a faint but definite smell, not a medicinal odor, but not one for a sachet, either. I put it in an old drawstring bag I had once used for odds and ends of laces and bindings and went to wash my hands. I knew what I had to do.

I had intended to pay a visit to the widow Riddell the next day on my way home from my round of errands, but Josie needed help with Anna, who was complaining of various aches and pains.

"She say someone sticking pins and needles into her legs and arms, ma'am," Josie said. "An' she don' look good. She be quiet, though, no screamin' an' yellin' like sometimes."

"I could send Maggie for Dr. Peterson," I said, "but—"

"No, no," Josie interrupted. "She have a fit when she see him, kick and bite. She tell me no doctor. You come see her, please, ma'am."

Anna did not look well; her thin face had a grayish tinge to it, and her eyes looked dull.

"Oh, Marike," she cried as soon as she saw me, "what have I done to deserve this? Demons, that's what they are, devils and demons sticking needles into me. Look, here's where . . ."

She pulled up the sleeve of her cotton nightdress and held out a thin, smooth white arm for me to inspect.

"See all the marks?" she asked excitedly. "They bleed, and they sting. Oh, how they hurt me! I can't stand the pain!"

"Josie, fetch a soft cloth and a basin of warm water, and put a few drops of my lavender essence in it," I said. "That should help. Yes, Anna, we'll rid you of the demons. Now, let me see your legs. Ah, I see. Don't you worry, Anna; demons and devils don't like sweet-smelling water and will disappear at once. You'll see. Now lie still. That's it."

For some reason my homemade cure worked like magic. By the time we'd finished bathing and drying Anna's arms and legs she'd drifted off to sleep. Josie went downstairs to cook up a pot of Anna's favorite soup while I sat next to the bed wondering how much longer we were to be responsible for this poor, sick, crazy woman. Her mother had been a burden to her for years, I mused; I guessed it was my turn now.

When Philip came home he insisted that we take some kind of action and sent for Dr. Peterson. As Josie had predicted, Anna kicked, screamed, and protested so violently when he tried to examine her that the visit was a total waste of time.

"I can tell you two things," the doctor said before he left. "Her color indicates that her heart is bad, and it is obvious that her mind is affected. If you cannot bring yourselves to send her to the asylum you must keep a close watch on her. She has the strength of a maniac and could do herself and others harm. There is always opium to quiet such cases, but I do not like to use it except as a last resort."

"Are we to live out our lives with a lunatic under our roof?" Philip asked when the doctor had gone. "Or do we send her to certain death in the asylum? If we keep her here the burden falls on you, Marike. I am away all day, but you: oh, think! There must be a way out of this. And what about Margretta and Adrien? They're young and shouldn't have to live with a crazy aunt."

"Maybe she isn't crazy," I said. "Perhaps she has what my

mother used to call 'spells' and gets excited and upset. I can't see Anna hurting anyone."

"But Peterson said—"

"I heard what he said, but I don't know that I believe him. Why don't we wait, Philip, wait a while and watch her, and then if things get too bad maybe I could take her to Ossining—oh, no—I couldn't ask Tante Greta to take care of her. Oh, dear, oh, I don't know."

We went to bed knowing nothing had been solved, and neither of us slept well that night.

Three days later Josie came to me with the news that Anna was sitting up in the armchair next to her window writing a letter.

"She's better today, ma'am," she said with a smile. "An' she tole me the demons and devils be all gone. She ate her porridge and bread and jam and drank her tea. She really be better. You go out; Josie will take care of things, and Maggie's here to help."

I was glad to be out in the cool freshness of the August morning (it had rained the night before, and everything looked bright and clean), with the sun just warm enough on my back and a cloudless blue sky stretched out above me. I felt encouraged by Josie's report and my step was lighter than it had been in several days as I made my way past Collect Pond to the widow's cottage.

"Come in, come in," she called in response to my knock. "Come in, it's open."

She was sitting in front of a little shelf sorting seeds or beans or some such and squinted slightly when she looked up at me

"Ah, yes," she said. "I remember. Where is your little girl? The one who liked my parrot?"

We talked for a few minutes about my children and after a while she asked what she could do for me. I remembered the tea that Josie had given me that dreadful night at Miss Peg's house, and asked the widow if she had some that would ensure a good night's sleep.

"I haven't slept very well lately," I said, "and wondered if you had some herb I could put in my tea to help me sleep."

"Ah, yes," she said readily. "Here is a packet of tea, all mixed with my secret herbs. You will sleep well if you drink a cup of this. I keep it for some ladies. You try it and you'll see how good it is."

I nodded, and then she began to ask about the Bogardus family. "Now tell me," she said, putting aside her bowl of seeds, "the lady who used to come here, Miss Anna, I think, where is she now? And the old lady, the one I made the potion for?"

When I told her that Mrs. Bogardus had died she shook her head, murmuring something about old age and then asking me if I wanted some of the potion for myself.

"No, thank you, but I am curious about this," I said, taking the pewter cup out of the drawstring bag. "Can you tell from the smell what it contained? Mrs. Bogardus was drinking from it just before she died."

"Let me see," she said, reaching for the cup and holding it up to her nose. "Not my potion, but rum, yes, rum and wait, wait."

She sat back in her chair, and as she sniffed again and again a look of horror appeared on her face. Finally she placed the cup on the end of the shelf nearest to me, and taking a clean cloth from the rack behind her, wiped her hands thoroughly.

"You should wash that in boiling water before you use it," she said slowly.

"What is it?" I asked. "What was in it that smells like that?"

"The poison I gave the lady for the rats," she answered. "It was never meant to be put in a cup."

"What poison? Which lady? Mrs. Bogardus?" I had trouble following her.

"No, not the old lady," the widow answered calmly. " 'Twas the daughter, Miss Anna, who came for it. Yes, indeed, I gave her henbane and nightshade, and when she said how afraid of rats she was I put in some arsenic, arsenico, I call it, just to be sure they would die quickly."

Maybe it was Saunders who gave it to Mrs. Bogardus, I thought in desperation. He could have. . . .

"And the old lady drank from this?" I heard the widow gasp in horror.

"I don't know," I said shakily. "I found the cup on the floor. Maybe it was put out for a rat and got knocked over."

"One dead rat for sure," she said, turning back to her shelf. "You be sure to wash that good, now."

I said I would, and after paying for the tea and buying a jar of ointment for itching skin (for Anna) I thanked her and took my leave.

The sun still shone and the sky was still bright blue, but nevertheless the day seemed to have darkened as I walked slowly down to the docks. I watched two ships go by and when they were out of sight I hurled the pewter cup as far as I could into the sun-dappled waters of the East River.

Chapter Twenty-four

S everal days went by before I could decide how to tax Anna—
or through her, Saunders—with the death of Mrs. Bogardus. I was afraid that any resurrection of the past might
bring on what Josie called "one of them fits." Anna had been quite
docile since the demons and devils left her, spending most of her
time writing long, impassioned letters to Hugh Saunders and giving those she didn't destroy to Josie to post.

I read one of them, a pathetic declaration of everlasting love,
full of endearments and reminders of how happy they had been.
It was almost heartbreaking to read sentences like the following:
"Hugh dearest, my only love, I know you'll come back to me soon
and carry me off to your estates, where we will be happy together
forever and ever. Come soon, my love, come soon."

This longing for the return of Saunders, repeated over and
over again, of course made no sense, since we'd told her I don't
know how many times that he'd fallen overboard and drowned
on his way to England. She simply refused to believe us, and in
a way it was just as well that she did, since writing endless let-

ters seemed to keep her happy. She seldom left her room during those letter-writing days, and Josie told me that the widow's tea, which she brewed for her every evening, ensured a good night's sleep, a blessed relief for everyone.

Perhaps I should have left well enough alone, but I didn't. I was sitting with Anna one rainy afternoon when she surprised me by saying that what she'd really like to have was a cup of the potion her mother used to drink.

"I'd have to go to the widow's for it, Anna," I said, "and it's a nasty day. The rain is coming down hard."

"Oh, I could go, Marike," she said quickly. "You know how often I used to go for Mama. I know the way."

"I know you do, Anna, and I remember how often you went there. But tell me, are you the one who bought the poison for the rats from the widow? I never saw any rats in that house."

"Oh, yes, yes. I needed it, you see. Once I'd made up my mind that Louisa had to die I had to have it. It's easy to kill someone, Marike, so easy . . ."

"Why did Louisa have to die, Anna?" I asked in as conversational a tone as I could manage.

"Oh, I thought you knew. She was flirting with Hugh. She shouldn't have done that. He belonged to me. But she did, and I could see that he liked it. She was so pretty, and I saw the way he looked at her."

"So you put the poison into the potion and gave it to Louisa to drink after she was in bed? She liked the taste of the potion, I know, because every once in a while I'd see her taking a sip of it."

"Yes, she did," Anna agreed with a sly smile. "That's why it was so easy. She almost grabbed the cup from me, and later when

I was sure she'd drunk it I went in and covered her face with the pillow, and nobody ever knew."

"And what about your mother? Did Hugh give her the drink that killed her?"

"Oh, no, Marike. Hugh wouldn't do that. He said he wouldn't, even when I told him how easy it was, and he laughed when I said I had the rat poison hidden in the toe of one of my old boots."

"So it was you."

"Yes, and Hugh never knew I gave it to her. I'd been waiting to do it for years, and when I found out we were leaving for Canada I thought the time had come, and that no one would ever know. I mixed the poison into her potion just before we left and gave it to her. I told her I'd be right back. And now it's too late to do anything about it, isn't it?"

I couldn't speak. I could hardly bring myself to nod as she repeated the question. Hugh Saunders was a thief and a scoundrel, but he was not a murderer. Anna was.

Or am I? Had I said something about what the widow said the day I took Margretta with me—just before we went to Ossining, it was—would two lives have been spared? Am I as guilty as Anna? Can silence be the eighth deadly sin?

Margretta

M y mother never added anything to those last poign-
ant lines in the papers she left hidden in the false
bottom of a locked drawer in her dressing table. I
found them when Pa asked me to sort out her clothing and possessions after her death in the fall of 1810. He said he couldn't
bear to go through her things. I have read what she wrote, but
I have not shown it to anyone yet. I am afraid they might need-
lessly upset my father, and in any case, they were addressed to
me, and me alone.

All I can add to what Mama wrote is this: I remember that
when Tanka brought Adrien and me back from Ossining at the
end of the summer of 1789 we were warned never to go into Aunt
Anna's room and to tiptoe past her door in case she was sleeping.
The two of us saw little of my aunt, but we knew that she kept
Mama and Josie busy until she either jumped or fell from the
window in her room and broke her neck on the stone path below.
She had left a note on her bed saying her lover was waiting for
her in the garden, but I did not know that until I was older.

Adrien and I were told she had gone for a walk in the moonlight and tripped over a stray dog or cat. We never missed her.

After that our house was far more cheerful than it had been when she was alive. I remember seeing my mother and father smiling and laughing across the dinner table instead of looking worried while they listened for sounds from the floor above. The shadow that Aunt Anna's presence had cast over all of us was gone, gone for good, and replaced by a warm, bright light.

Had Mama lived she would have been pleased with the course, or courses, our lives have taken: Great-uncle Franz had left the Ossining property to her, and then it passed to my father. Pa has sold the Elizabeth Street house and the chandlery and now lives in the old farmhouse with Tanka. "I always thought I'd like to own a farm, Margretta," he said to me one day, "and look what has happened! Now in my old age I have one and can do as much or as little as I please. It is beautiful here; your mother loved it. Just look at the light of the sun on the pear trees and the shadows cast by the giant oaks!"

The last time I was there he gave me the little silver ring Mama always wore, even though she had several finer ones that he'd bought her over the years. "She wanted you to have it, my daughter," he said with a smile. "She said it would bring you happiness." I think it has.

I love going up to the farm for a visit each summer with our children, sure of a warm welcome from Pa and from Tanka. Dear Tanka! He still calls me "little one" after all these years. . . .